BOOK 1

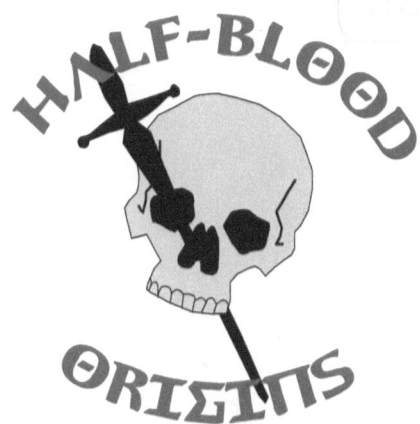

HALF-BLOOD

ORIGINS

THE BOOK OF
SHADOWS

RUSTY WISSMAN III

To my Mom and Dad,
for always encouraging me to keep
reading, and writing

CONTENTS

Half-Blood Origins: Book of Shadows

CHAPTER 1

IT ALL STARTED WHEN I WAS BORN

Usually you can get a hero to give you an awesome origin story, but that is not my style, nor the cases. My name is Kyle Pierce, and I am not your normal hero. For starters, I am a demigod. I am a Son of Poseidon and the grandson of Athena. My mom was a daughter of Athena and trained under Chiron and now I take after her and do the same routine she grew up with. I am currently 16 years old and attend Demigod Central, in the Realms.

Yeah that's right I said Chiron. You know the dude who trained Hercules, Achilles, and all the other great heroes of the ancient times. Chiron is a centaur, which is half-human from the waist up and well half-horse waist down. Chiron was originally harsh to me, but several years ago he warmed up when I was finally put into a group.

So I was born in a hospital like everyone else, except there were complications with my birth, and sadly my mother died while giving birth to me. Chiron took me in, and well, he acted like a father to me. Well if a father wakes you up at 3 A.M. to do combat training when he's free. But yeah, its cool I'm a demigod that can kick ass! Please don't tell

Chiron I said that he will hunt me down and I'll get dish duty for a week.

When I was 7 I learned there was a prophecy that would shape my life, friends, who I can trust, and all of that good stuff. As a gift from the gods, to assist me in the task of saving them, each one blessed me with a talent when I was first born. Zeus gave me the ability to shift the wind. Sorta, still learning how to use this, but really it is not helpful and is pretty weak. Hades gave me my weapon named Shadow. It's a two handed blade, forged from the River Styx and can pierce any metal known to man.

Demeter gave me the ability to know my whereabouts on land. Really, really helpful, if I was allowed on Earth! Athena blessed me with intelligence. Don't have to try hard in school, so obviously I like this one!

Aphrodite blessed me with good looks. Hey can't complain! Dionysus gave me a butt-ton of wine, but I can't touch it until I turn 21. I'm ninety-nine percent sure Chiron's been drinking it to put up with me for these past 16 years.

Hermes gave me the gift of stealth, and that's been handy here on campus for sneaking around past curfew. I can sneak past the demons that lurk the halls. Chiron you did not just hear that.

Apollo gave me the gift of music and Artemis gave me the ability of dead on accuracy in archery. I can hit a bullseye from 103 yards away. Do not get me to try 104 because I will miss 100% of those shots. Remember these powers have limits.

Hephaestus gave me the gift of skilled crafting so I don't botch up my work in the Bunker. Ares gave me the gift of skilled fighting, which comes in hand while training with Chiron. And well of course I get my natural powers from my dad over water, hydrokinesis as some wish to call it.

My school life was alright. I did well in my classes, never getting less than a B+. And I was a jock in all the events the school held. A sophomore who could kick-erhhhh I won't say it again incase Chiron is around. But yeah, I kicked everyone's butt.

My friends were pretty cool too. There's Gwen, daughter of Demeter, who was one of my best friends growing up. There's Brian Schmitz, son of the Sun god. He is of Native-American lineage. Long story behind his lineage. He mentioned something about it possibly being Wi, but not like the Nintendo Console, although it would be cool to be the son of the god of video games.

Brian had an older brother, named Joey Schmitz. I had always admired Joey for his bravery on quests and adventuring skills. He was awesome, and I wish I could go on a true quest with him one day.

However, Charles Akbar, the school dean, always ruled against me leaving campus due to safety concerns, and for my well-being. Mostly since an incident a few years back.

I never understood why until that one fateful quest that had ripped my life out of my grasps. That awful truth that would leave a burden upon me. I'll recount that event. But only this once, and nevermore, for this changed my life permanently, and not in the good way.

Where should I start this story? The time I came face to face with a gorgon, nah. How about the riverside tale? Too cliché. Here, I'll use this one, Bunker 4921. That'll be where this story will start. The first sequence of events that lead to this cursed errand of a quest for a useless book.

***

It was a Saturday night earlier this year and I was sitting in our group, Bunker 4921, and I stared blankly at the book we had by Livy. I had enjoyed reading his version of history. This dude basically just sat there and said, "Look, I don't really care if it is fact or myth. Good enough for our ancestors, it's good enough for us!" I thoroughly enjoyed that kind of logic. I had just reread the tale of Romulus and Remus and the founding of Rome, the beginning of an empire. The two were descendants of Venus and were both children of Mars. Great combination of blood for a hero.

Anyways back to my point. The Bunker was filled with useless junk. Scraps of sheet metal hung on the walls, useless paintings tossed in the corner. Two young twins, 8 years old, sat in the corner playing with LEGO's. They were way too advanced working on the larger, more advanced kits and even building a replica of Demigod Central.

I envied them not having to worry about monsters and this destiny I supposedly had. They were going to have a mostly normal childhood, or at least for a demigod.

Joey sat at the table rubbing his head. He had a dark tan skin complexion. His hair was short, dark, and brushed to the side. He had a tattoo on his left arm of a skull with a dagger through it. I stared at the skull momentarily as its empty eye sockets were always captivating, as if trying to suck me in.

It caught my attention and I couldn't break its spell. I put down the book and ventured to the table. He was drawing up a plan with two other members of Bunker 4921. We were the smallest unit at Demigod Central, but also one of the most elite. Which was good in a sense. It meant everyone got to know one another very quickly. But on the down side our training was intense. And I usually skipped it.

I remember when I was first inducted into the Bunker I had to do a training sequence as an initiation process. Nobody ever told me I'd be fighting a real monster. And not just a monster, several. That's right, the plural of it, monsters! I fought 4 hellhounds, a manticore, and a gargoyle all at once. Which can I say is not cool in any standards.

***

There I was standing in the arena. The sand floor had my old beat up sneakers digging into it. As though it was quicksand I knew that me being quick on my feet was not going to be likely today. Then just like back in Ancient Rome, in the Colosseum, the gate raised up unveiling the beasts.

I was only expecting to face one monster, but instead the

four hellhounds busted out of the gate. They lined the ring of the arena. I knew I was going to have to think fast with four hellhounds. And just then I realized the gate had yet to close.

"Oh you've got to be kidding me," I grumbled as a gargoyle riding a manticore walked out of the gate. With a clash the gate slammed shut. Each beast had their own fair share of growls and snarls towards me. Then one of the hellhounds made the first move. I had somehow managed to take it down on its first strike. Shadow had slashed through it like butter.

"Nice!" I smoldered to myself. Then the second hellhound jumped me slamming me on my back snapping at my face. My sword's blunt edge was pressed against its neck. The only thing preventing it from killing me on the spot.

The hellhound then knocked my sword out with a slash of its paw. I grabbed its neck and the hellhound grappled with me momentarily. I had to snap the hound's neck and push it off of me in order to progress my fight.

My leather armor was now scratched and damaged pretty bad. I watched the big pile of rocks that was the gargoyle, jump off the manticore like nothing. I kept eye contact with it just in case it made a sudden move towards me. I then readjusted my focus to see the manticore raise its tail to fire off a round of spiked quills. I stupidly ran towards the gargoyle and used him as a shield. I used my sword, Shadow, to push him backwards and at bay until he tripped on the manticore crushing it. I then spun around in a rage slashing and killing a third hellhound. All I needed to do now was kill the last hellhound and the gargoyle and my induction would be complete.

The last hellhound was hiding somewhere, but that somewhere was out of my direct line of sight. I began to panic as I had looked down seeing blood. I was kind of afraid of blood, and well the sight of my own blood began to make me queasy. Apparently that one hellhound did scratch me and got me good enough through the leather armor. No wonder the Romans abandoned the concept of leather armor. I looked around as the gargoyle began to rise from the crushed manticore. "You know what would be funny big guy?" I said in a sarcastic manner feeling confident.

The faceless rock man scratched his head, "What?"

"Killing that last monster for me. Yeah, that'd be great." I smiled and waited for him to react.

"Not a chance runt!" His voice was so deep and brooding it had me shaking. A gargoyle's voice was definitely up there in my top ten menacing voice list.

"Drat, I was hoping you could." He swung his fist at me knocking my sword clean from my hands. "I did not plan on that happening."

My jaw dropped as I gawked at the enraged gargoyle advancing on me. As I paced backwards I had tripped on a dead hellhound in the arena and landed on my butt. I scuttled backwards in a desperate frenzy to somehow get out of his way. Too late...

My hand had gone backwards helping me crab walk right

into a puddle of drool. I tilted my head backwards to see the hellhound snarling at me. My eyes widen as I started to panic. What else could I do? I was about to die in my training sequence.

Just then an arrow pierced through the hellhound's skull and three more stuck to the gargoyle. "Haha. Puny arrows do no damage." He pulled them out with ease and snapped them in half. Wait arrows? Where on Hades name did they come from?

Into the arena slid a masked archer with a quiver on his back and his bow in his hands. "Hey stonewall buddy. Over here." Whoever this kid was he was gutsy. "C'mon! You know you wanna get some payback don't ya!"

He smirked as the gargoyle took the bait. I scuttled over to my sword still keeping an eye on the archer in case he decided to turn on me. The archer snapped his bow and light flew out of it. It was now in two, one and half foot gold and ivory blades. Chryselephantine was the word! Ha, I did know something. Half gold and half ivory. Whoever this archer was he was skilled in a fight.

He slashed at the gargoyle and split him into two easily. He twirled the blades and it was once again a bow. He flung it over his shoulder and approached me. His mask was a balaclava with two eye slits. The stitching on it was gold and patchy. "Welcome to Bunker 4921," he said as he walked closer to me. "My name's Nightbow."

I looked at him confused, "Nightbow? No, it's not. You're wearing a mask it's probably your alias that you go by. What's your real name?"

Nightbow chuckled, "Hm, my alias, maybe it will catch on, one day. Anyways," he said taking off his mask, "The name is really Brian Schmitz. I'll be your new roommate. My brother is Joey Schmitz, the leader of our Bunker."

I took his hand and he hefted me to my feet. Once I was on my feet, he stared me in the eyes and I did the same. His eyes were like a golden brown and his skin complexion was tanned. He had a smoldered look across his face as he looked at me. He was just barely shorter than me and I had only about an inch on him.

That was how I had met Brian Schmitz, my best friend.

Later that night, at dinner, I had met Gwen Mahoney for the first time as well. Across the table from Brian sat, Gwen Mahoney, daughter of Demeter. She was definitely an interesting ally and friend.

Her light brown hair swept down past her shoulders. A blue ribbon was laced through her hair. She had a dimple on her left cheek. She decided to mimic all of my actions that night as well. She had finally made me lose my cool and I drew Shadow on her. I remember how she just glanced up from her plate smirking and she said, "I win."

I looked at her, "Won what?" I was now confused I thought she was just copying my movements not in some psychological game. I lowered my sword and had I had begun to stare at her intently trying to make my own analysis.

"In any fight you and I ever undertake, I would win. You are cocky and rash. You do not take in subtlety, or at least if you do it is by no means a strong suit of yours."

My jaw had dropped and Brian leaned in as I sat back down in my seat, "Oooohhh, she just owned you."

Joey looked at me and just chuckled, "Guess you just met the Bunker's second newest member, Gwen Mahoney." She was one of the original trio in the Bunker

As if on cue she stood and bowed. I smirked at her as she did so.

Although Gwen and myself bickered at first, we eventually grew close and bonded as friends. Heck, now I'd say we are best friends. Brian, Gwen, and myself an inseparable trio nowadays.

***

"We physically cannot do this as a plan, unless you are trying to get us all seriously injured Joey." Gwen stared at the map with intent. A few streaks of her light brown hair fell across her forehead. She saw me as I approached the table and she pulled out a chair for me next to her.

I sat down and studied the strategy. It showed the Bunker 4921 teamed up with a few other squads. The whole concept of squads kind of rubbed me the wrong way. In my opinion we should just train as a group and together. Not individuals. For this event we would be teamed up with larger squads, which made sense since we were the smallest at Demigod Central. Joey had a mock draft of who would be on our side for this event: The Grecian Spartans, The Wildcards, and Stop, Hammer Time.

"The Stop, Hammer Time group is with us again?" I asked in a bit of protest. The past three events that they were teamed up with us they did what their name says, STOP. They let the other team walk right into our zone and capture the orb. They literally dropped their weapons when they saw him. Then again this was the fire wielding son of Poseidon. My cousin could control fire since he was a legacy child. Me, no, my legacy is intelligence and wit thanks to my grandma, Athena. No offense grandma.

"Headmaster Akhbar paired everyone together for this one. He claims some special visitor is coming for this game. He made a mention that she wants to see how certain people interact with others."

Brian looked like an anxious dog ready to go to the bathroom. He sat across the table with his right arm raised and his left arm acting as a support beam. Gwen began squinting her eyes at him like, Really? Do you not have any self-control? I looked at Brian myself now. He was now bouncing in his seat. Joey was refusing to respond to his little brother's childish behavior. Jim finally spoke up from the other room, "Hey, Joey?"

"Yes," Joey said in response to the younger twin.

"Brian wants to say something. Either that or he wet himself again."

Brian's hand slammed against the table knocking a few of

the pieces off of their original location on the map. "I did not wet myself anytime recently for your information!"

"Then what are you so impatient about now then?" Joey asked in annoyance.

Brian paused and tried to recall, "Oh yeah! Could I go grab an ice cream from the freezer?" Gwen and Joey both slapped their faces and just looked at him with disgust. "I'll take that as a yes!"

He scampered off to the kitchen. I picked up one of the pieces and adjusted it to where I thought Joey had had it. Apparently I had moved it in a drastic way. Joey surveyed the map. "What's this that you've done?"

"Uh, just fixing it. Didn't you have the South section fortified by the Wildcards?"

"No but that gives them a useful purpose. Good job Kyle!"

Gwen stood up in protest, "Wait, what about the idea I was proposing? Having the Wildcards focus their attention to the Northeast."

"No need Gwen. It provides for more assault for us and an opportunity to corner them if they get to far in. Good job Kyle. Now let's go eat." He patted me on my back as he walked over to gather the twins and leave for dinner.

The only ones left in the Bunker's strategy room was Gwen and myself. She looked at me with fierce eyes for a daughter of a Demeter. I gave her a quick smile and just laughed.

"I can't believe you stole my thunder."

My face dropped from happiness to a bit of annoyance, "Hey, I'm a child of the ocean. We got thundering waves."

"Arrogant."

"Excuse me?" I asked in a bit of confusion.

"You always need to be the best. Your ego is dangerously high. Just keep that in mind for when you are in the field one day. You let your guard down, the enemy will eat that up. What is more important you're one of my greatest friends. I don't want to lose you either."

I bowed my head blushing and looked back up at Gwen. Gosh she was stunningly beautiful. "You don't need to worry. I've handled myself before. Besides, Chiron isn't even positive its about me yet."

"Your stupidity has you sold for a fool. You're so naive. You would walk right up to the enemy and say, Hey look. I'm right here! Come kill me! And you act like no one would care."

"You seem upset."

"I'll see you at dinner Kyle." She grabbed her running jacket off the back of her chair and made her way for the elevator.

I plopped down in the chair and looked around the now empty bunker. I figured I might as well get some rest before dinner so I took a little nap. Except the word little was an understatement, a large understatement.

CHAPTER 2

THE INFLICTOR

My dream started simple enough. I guess a usual dream. Is there a special name for normal dreams? Dreams that go wrong are nightmares, so I guess a normal dream is what I had.

I sat alongside a beach. Each wave lapped against the beach as if it was high-fiving the sand. I had in my hand a lemonade, my favorite drink. Chiron once had made a punch card for me to limit how many lemonades I could get in a week from the cafeteria. I saw a boy and a girl running off in the distance playing tag it seemed. They were blurry so I couldn't make out many of their features out except the brown hair.

I laid back against the sand, resting my head on a pillow I had made out of it. I closed my eyes and was at peace with myself. I was calm and tranquil. I had found a happy spot.

Then the scene changed.

My eyes fluttered open and the sun glistened against the water. But it was not the same water. This was some fresh water pond. My hand was shaking. Sweat beaded across my forehead. As I stood up and turned my back to the pond, across the road sat a gas station's convenience store.

My hand, which wasn't my hand, began to write,

Each day passes slowly. I am not pleased of what I am tasked to do.

The people and things that they are requesting now are becoming harder

to convince. I fear as though force will become more and more common,

but this is now my job. And I must abide to it. I'll report more

in the log tomorrow. Until then...

The journal closed swiftly and I put it in the satchel that I was wearing. After quickly examining my surroundings and my body from what I could see, I noted that I was in the body of some brute of a force. The body of a brick wall.

I, or whoever I was now, walked across the street and into the store. We looked around for a bit until coming across two 17 year olds, a guy and a girl. The young adults slowly backed up and the guy said, "Why are you back? I thought we gave you an answer."

Whoever I was apparently gave a crooked smile to them, "Alas you did. But now I have another question for you boy. What did you say your name was again?"

The guy looked hesitant but he finally spoke, "Hector. Why does it matter?"

"Because, Hector, I am going to share with you and your sweet darling of a friend a story about what happen when a girl a bit younger than you all crossed the Legion."

The girl stood forward in a ready to fight stance, "I'm not scared of you!"

The man chuckled and rolled up the sleeves of his shirt. "No, not many people need to feel fear to join us. Our original recruiter, now he was a legend. He would just approach you, and BAM you would be sold. Nope. Not the modern demigod. You all have to be swayed by fear itself. Or a loss."

"A loss?" asked the girl.

"I'm sorry miss. I'm bad with names. What was yours again?"

"Vivian," she said with a quiver in her voice as if she was resenting saying her name.

"You're strong Vivian. But not compelled yet to join us. See you, unlike your boyfriend here, are willing to feed on more power. You have conviction."

The man drew a sword and tapped a mark on his arm. "This is who you will be fighting for from here on Vivian. You're one of us now." He looked at the guy once more, "I truly am sorry, but it's my job. And well duty calls."

He swung his sword and sliced Hector in the middle of the chest. He took out a pocket hanky stained with dried blood of his past victims and wiped the blade of the dripping blood. Vivian dropped to her knees crying draped against his fallen body. Blood began to puddle around his crumpled body.

"I'm sorry Vivian. I truly am. But there is no convincing

certain demigods. But we needed the daughter of Hecate alive regardless. Welcome to the Legion of Tartarus, Vivian."

Hector was critically wounded and he wouldn't last much longer. She wiped her eyes and looked up for a brief moment. "Who, who are you?"

He just pulled out a pair of sunglasses and put them on his face as he began to walk out the door, "Just call me the Inflictor. I'll be in touch." With that the Inflictor handed her a parchment of old paper. Papyrus, I believe. And on it was an incantation. Vivian looked at it intently for a moment. She knew exactly what this incantation was.

I had realized I was no longer attached to that guy, the Inflictor. I was a free floating being, like a ghost. I peaked over Vivian's shoulder attempting to read it. All I saw was what appeared to be a bunch of lines and squiggles. This is what I saw:

Vivian studied it for another moment as she knelt down next to Hector. She placed her hand on the wound and began to murmur something. But whatever she said worked.

Hector's eyes began to flutter open "Wha-what happened? Vivian are you ok?" He was in a bit of a frenzy.

"Hector it's ok," she said reassuring him. "That guy said he was the Inflictor. He helped me save you. He gave me this."

She showed him the incantation. "Vivian this isn't good. We were supposed to run from this guy. Now we are going to join him?"

Vivian diverted her eyes away from his, "I am. You should come along."

"The Legion of Tartarus is our enemy, Vivian. We can't just side with them."

"We have to at this point Hector, I have to at least. If he has more incantations, I need them. I'm drawn to power and he's offering it up. I'm not going to be a fool and pass this opportunity off."

At this point I felt like I didn't belong in this conversation any more. Some girlfriend/boyfriend drama was going down, and well yeah, I didn't wanna be in the middle of it.

"Vivian you've seen what they can do. I'm sorry but, I am not joining the Legion. I'm going to find this portal we were told about, and go find Demigod Central. I'm the son of Hermes, not some spell caster. If you find our enemy more appealing then farewell."

Vivian just stood there as Hector grabbed his bag and began to walk away. He didn't look back at her. Not once.

Her lip quivered but she didn't falter. She was set on her choice as he was set on his. She watched as he left. She looked back at the parchment of an incantation and stuffed it in her back pocket. She walked toward the checkout counter and put her beverage and candy bar on it to pay for it.

I began to loose focus on the scene. As if the two were my signal strength, and as they parted it broke up the connection. My dream began to fade as white noise began to fill my ears. Static came across the scene as my sight began to fail. I slowly began to wake up from this dream what seemed to be a nightmare.

CHAPTER 3

DINNER GETS A VISITOR

I woke up with a start as a cold sweat beaded on my forehead. I had just fallen out of my seat and fallen to the slab of a floor that we had in the Bunker. *Wait!* What in Hades name, had I just witnessed? Some half-blood named Hector getting maimed, and another, oh gosh what was her name, Vivian? Yeah, Vivian, was just healing him with magic from some book?

Whatever, some daughter of Hecate was now part of some group with some evil guy who called himself the Inflictor.

I rubbed the tiredness out of my eyes. "Oh gosh, what am I getting myself into now." I yawned to fully wake up and glanced over at the clock. "Aw crap!" It was 7:15 PM.

Dinner usually starts at 6:30 and goes until 7:45. We get all the announcements for the day and upcoming news for the next, the usual banter from Chiron, and well then we eat. But now I would just be straight up late.

I knew instantly that Chiron would give me grief the next morning at our early training session. I felt my heart sink a bit as I walked into the cafeteria. I had missed gyro night!

"You're late," Joey said scolding as I slid into my seat at the table. I didn't want to give Joey the satisfaction of rubbing it in that I was late. He knew exactly where I was.

Brian slid me a plate of food. I gave him a nod of gratitude. I took less than one bite of the succulent meat when I heard the microphone being tapped.

"Is this infertile contraption working?" echoed a voice softly throughout the cafeteria.

"Uhm, yes madam," Chiron muttered.

"Ah good." The voice was like a melodic lullaby. "Welcome Demigods or, more like thank you for hosting me tonight, and these next few nights. I am Hestia, goddess of the Hearth."

Whatever food was in my hand at the time, fell to the plate and splattering against my clothes. An Olympian was here! My chance to finally go on a quest could be at hand. I could go on my own journey and experience the world. We could end the Bunker's funk of not being permitted to explore the Realms.

"This Friday, as many of you are aware of, the school shall host its monthly game. This month's game is Pirate Ball." There was a scattered murmurs erupting from various groups. The last time Demigod Central had played Pirate Ball was several years ago. They had abandoned it as a game after a half-blood had been seriously maimed by some son of Jupiter.

Actually not just some son of Jupiter, the son of Jupiter. He was the leader of the Legionnaires, a strictly Roman demigod elite group. The Legionnaires house the top 50 Roman demigods and well, that son of Jupiter, Phil Stryker. This kid was 17, just a year older than me but he acted like he was the best in the world. It annoyed me to all get out. I'm a legacy myself but this kid, Phil, he was a power house. He was the son of the king of the gods, Jupiter himself. But on top of that his mom was a demigod child of Aeolus, king of the winds. So a Grecian Roman, ok I can work with this. But nope, it gets better! His mother was also trained or part of the Egyptian's, so she had Egyptian skills in her blood. That gives this kid extreme power over the sky and magic too. Can you say overpowered. I'm sorry Phil but it's true.

Well four years ago, this fall, Phil was out with the Legionnaires. He was one of the best. I remember this because, I saw Phil take down Calvin the son of Dionysus with his lightning.

I was on Calvin's team and I spotted him assaulting the Legionnaires base. He was close to the orb when Phil spotted him. Phil drew his weapon, a dice he called Aureus. He had rolled the dice and it had landed on the number 1. It shifted into a gladius but Calvin struck swiftly and disarmed Phil. Enraged Phil screamed and his eyes went dark. A storm began to rage around us. I wasn't as harshly buffed by the wind due to Zeus' blessing but Calvin took a beating. After the wind a dark flash immersed itself into Phil and redirected into Calvin. A dark lightning bolt, so powerful it sent me flying off my feet, and I slipped into unconsciousness. I get knocked out cold a lot.

When I slowly began to regain consciousness, I recalled Chiron standing over a broken Calvin and scolding Phil. The game had been cut short due to the incident.

I had never talked to Phil, but when I stood up he had shot me a glance. He knew who I was, and he wanted to test my power. He apparently tests anyone who thinks they can beat him. And he usually proves his opponent wrong.

I was brought back to reality when I saw Phil Stryker standing up on his table applauding Hestia. "Bravo! Bravo! Great game choice lady Vesta."

Hestia looked down with annoyance at him. Several other kids began to laugh though. Joey bit his lip, as if he wanted to speak down to him and just berate him. Phil and I exchanged a glance and I then knew one thing was for certain, I would be watching out for Phil Stryker at the game this weekend.

Hestia's gaze narrowed in on the son of Jupiter. "For such a strong spawn of a Roman deity you lack common graces and knowledge. Maybe in time you will learn such simple things. Otherwise your mind shall stay cluttered of petty victories."

Listening to Hestia's words seemed to echo out across the dining hall. All had fallen silent in their revelries to gawk at Hestia's warning to Phil. She was one of the first people, erh goddess to put Phil in his place.

"The game will take place later this week and will be graced by guest appearances. Be prepared demigods for I sense this game will have weigh heavy on some of your futures."

As we all began to depart from dinner I spotted Phil looking at me. He put his finger to his throat and made a slicing motion and pointed at me. I swallowed the lump in my throat. Fear entered my body and began to flourish as it spread through my veins. He mouthed, "You're next!"

CHAPTER 4

TIME FOR A LESSON

The next day was a bit tiring and slow. The excitement of the news presented by Hestia at dinner had been circling in my mind. How would I fight Phil? How *could* I fight Phil! That was my main goal. To take down the arrogant son of Jupiter. Or you know, just survive the fight. Whichever was easier.

"Kyle, the answer please?" said my teacher in annoyance.

"17, Mr. Cato!" yelled Brian from across the room.

Mr. Cato rolled his eyes and glanced at Brian, "Is your name Kyle, Mr. Schmitz? No, good. I did not think it was."

Brian leaned his chair back against the wall and propped his feet on the desk, "I can be whoever you want me to be." He smiled and winked at Mr. Cato. The whole class could see annoyance radiating off of Mr. Cato's face as Brian smirked at him.

"Fine, if this is how you wish to act Brian, we will have some fun with your bantering. Keith, who is Brian the child of?"

Keith was the son of Hades. He didn't like to talk much let alone in this math class. "Uh, Wi."

Brian saw the opportunity and couldn't resist. "Oh Keith, I didn't know you spoke French!"

I wanted to walk back there and slap him in the face. He just sat there with a stupid grin on his face glaring at Mr. Cato. Mr. Cato pretended to not hear the comment.

Mr. Cato glared at the others in the room, "Fine, Ethan write your sentence for homework on the board. Maybe one of you will show some sort of improvement today, and we can actually call this dysfunctional place a school."

Ethan pushed his chair out, "Dysfunctional my butt. My homework is flawless as always." Ethan made his way to the board. See Ethan was an interesting kid. I didn't really know him, but I had to give the kid some credit, he was street smart, but he was not too book smart. This kid, well you'll see.

As he walked to the board he began to curse softly. He paused and repeatedly tapped his chalk against the board. "Ah, yeah," he faintly spoke. "You know what Mr. Cato, what if instead I just gave a quick report?"

Mr. Cato just shrugged his shoulders and gave in, "You know what, why not Ethan. I'd love to hear the convoluted history lesson I could possibly get from you."

Ethan smirked, "Oh, don't worry, I love this stuff." He turned to the class and began, "It all started when time began. The universe was ever expanding, and so were the thoughts of the world. Chaos and Order had formed in it. From this focus fell from the universe back to Earth, however with each possibility strung open the new universes. But these universes faded as the possibility was not an option."

Kids in the class began to laugh at Ethan and he took his seat. Mr. Cato stood up and rubbed his eyes in frustration, "Fine, you want the true story, here you go. And this is so far away from Math." He cleared his throat, "So at the dawn of humanity people have looked to higher beings for explanation. There belief grew so much that their thoughts became real. This resulted in the formation of the gods. When something can be so strongly believed in it had a possibility of forming. However, they could not coexist well on Earth. Over time people had tried to harm them and wage wars on them. This erupted in conflicts across the world and the gods choosing sides. Simple enough right? Well not quite. The gods from a civilization would begin to fade into a separate place, the Realms. So where Mount Olympus once stood just resides a mountain with no glorious kingdom at the top. Instead it resides in the Realms, like our campus, Demigod Central. We are built on the ruins of some old religion that is so far old their gods are dead."

The whole class shifted uncomfortably. Keith rose his hand hesitantly, "You're saying gods can die? As in like no longer exist?"

The room was silent, until Mr. Cato reluctantly answered his question, "Yes. If a god or goddess loses all remnants of their life on Earth they too become vulnerable. They can be wounded and killed like any of us."

I instantly had a memory of a place Chiron once took me. There was this island underground and it was surrounded by water. An old man sat on the beach with an old bow and a quiver with three arrows left. The beach was full of white sand and coconut trees. Further inland was a jungle, and if navigated that properly was a maximum security building. Chiron did not take me in to the building but he did tell me something special resided inside, a pillar. This pillar was supposed to help a myth from fading. Once it was talked about and remembered it would be magically carved into the pillar. It was like a totem in a sense. Oh what was it called, a Palladium!

My hand shot up like lightning strikes through the sky, "The palladiums of each myth. Those can prevent the gods from dying without people caring for them. It's like their immortality."

Chatter rose around the classroom. The teacher sat in fear. "Mr. Kyle Pierce! The Palladium is not to be talked about in casual. That story is just a myth. If something along that caliber existed, dangerous things would happen. That is just a myth." He looked at the clock and sat on his desk. "Class you all are dismissed. Kyle please come forward and talk to me for a minute after class."

The kids all scattered out of the room pushing past one another. I walked forward to Mr. Cato's desk. Brian tried to stay behind but Mr. Cato insisted he leave. So unfortunately

Brian had to go back to the bunker alone.

See going back to the bunker alone would usually mean much needed alone time. However today the twins did not have classes, so it meant babysitting. One babysitter for them was most certainly not enough either. We could use an army to try to keep them under control.

Mr. Cato coughed aggressively to get my attention. I had to do a double take to make sure he wasn't about to double over on me. He looked like he was ready to punch a brick wall, which we have seen him do before. "Look kid, how dare you speak of the Palladium." He had reached forward and grabbed a tight grip on my shirt collar. "You do not realize the threat yet, but we have been infiltrated, and they are in search of the Palladium. They seek to destroy the gods and they need that to do so."

"Well what are supposed to do learn incorrect history? I've been to where it's located."

Mr. Cato slammed me against the wall and his arm was pinning my neck to it. I was losing my ability to breath and started choking. "Now listen up you little delinquent. If you dare speak of, or search for these Palladiums I will make sure we stop you before letting the Legion get a hold of you!"

Just then Mr. Akhbar walked by the door and saw what was happening, "Mr. Cato!" he screamed in his British accent. "Release the child at once and see me in my office immediately!"

Reluctantly Mr. Cato let go of his grasp of me and he slipped a note into my pocket as he walked away. Mr. Akhbar looked at me and adjusted his collar, "Kyle continue and you will be reassigned to a different class shortly. I will talk to Chiron about it. Until then have a nice day."

I shuffled around and fixed my t-shirt. "Jackass," I murmured under my breath. But then I decided to check on what this note was exactly. Once I unfolded the note I saw a doodle. It was some skull with some sort of knife going through an eye socket. Written on the note in big red letters was, "BEWARE OF THE LEGION'S SIGN! TRUST ONLY A FEW!"

Well, I had officially stumbled upon the weirdest nut job this school could find. By the looks of it, they had found Mr. Paranoid. But I had seen this skull with a knife through it somewhere, but where?

The thought puzzled me, but I crumpled the note up and put it in my pocket as I walked out of class. Upon exiting I was ambushed by Gwen. "Howdy buddy!" She said smiling. "Get held up again? What trouble did you cause now?"

I smirked at her, "Yikes, if I had known I would be getting 101 questions I may have just stayed in there a bit longer. Where are you even coming from?"

"I was coming back from class when I saw Headmaster Akhbar walking away with your teacher. I saw Brian venture off somewhere ahead. He's probably stilling waiting for you from a safer distance."

I tried to think why Mr. Cato would warn me. Gwen was smart and trust worthy. No I couldn't let this bother me. He's a nut for crying out loud, what he was saying couldn't possibly be true. "Well, I guess we should catch up to Brian then."

We began to walk down the hallway together in our usual manner. We got near the elevator and I could hear Brian. We turned the corner and saw Phil staring down Brian.

Phil smiled at me, "Ah there he is! Just the man I wanted to see. The one who will get his own ass handed to him on a platter this weekend."

Brian pushed Phil back as he drew his bow and poised it at Phil, "You ready to put your money where your mouth is?"

Phil chuckled and pushed the arrow off of its guide on Brian's bow. "Amusing, but my quarrel is not with you, it is with your friend." Phil walked up to me. "Kyle, what shall I do with you come this weekend? Fry you up once you try to summon some water?"

I looked into his stone gaze. His eyes were fierce like lightning and I was pretty positive I saw sparks actually flickering off of him.

"Actually, I was planning on taking you to dinner and then giving you a nice can of whoop ass," I said calmly.

"Why I ought to," his threat was cut short as Brian had readied his bow again.

"Back down goldilocks," Brian commanded with a smile on his face.

Phil snickered at the three of us. "Just wait until your friends are not there to save your hide Pierce. Then you are mine!" He walked away laughing.

Brian swung his bow over his back and snapped the arrow in his hand in half. Gwen pushed the elevator button and the three of us walked into the elevator not knowing what to do.

CHAPTER 5

I TAKE TRAINING TO THE NEXT LEVEL

Gwen scanned her ID card against the elevator and we began our descent. Why didn't I just stand up more for myself? Instead I let Phil walk all over me, and Brian be my bodyguard.

Gwen began talking, "I believe we should build up a central defense around Kyle and not let him into the fray. Phil is just going to target him the entire time. In our area we can at least protect him."

"Are we playing the game or protect the president here?" Brian scoffed.

"Well, I don't want Kyle hurt here."

"Guys," I tried to interject, but they were too engaged with one another.

I paraded myself to the back of the Bunker and was shutting Gwen, and Brian out. I passed the common room and saw Joey on the couch reading a book. He looked up and was about to put his book down to come talk to me. I put my hand up and he got the message. Joey knew to let my temper be and let me be in my mood.

In marching to the back room I saw the twins. They were busy fiddling with some new invention. Their creations always intrigued me. These two were definitely a step up from normal kids building things. It was some sort of mechanical arm. Miniature, but a prototype. Jim began to tell me it was supposed to emit some kind of magic but they didn't know where to get the magic from.

I looked at Brian and Gwen who were talking about this upcoming game so I decided to listen in. "Oh of course it does Brian. This ruins everything." I glanced at Joey to see what he was doing but he had already shut the world out with his book.

"Well, we can't just send him lone wolf anymore. Especially with that one gunning for him."

I walked off into the armory. Gwen and Brian ended up following me. The two of them had a nervous look on their face. I looked against the walls for something to use. A knife? I wasn't to great when it came to close quarters combat. A bow? I personally had no idea how to aim one of those things really. Sure I could shoot really far, but it was all luck. I gave Brian credit for being skilled with his bow and short swords.

Gwen looked at me sternly for a moment without saying anything. Once I finally looked her in the eyes she spoke up, "Kyle, you and your rage need to calm down. Just because Phil got inside your head doesn't mean you have to let it show."

"Plus you might not have to fight him alone!" Brian chided in.

I looked at him like, *what do you mean not alone?* He had managed to throw me off with that comment. What did he think I wouldn't fight Phil at all? Cause sure as hell I was going to fight him. Jupiter against Poseidon. Storm versus water. I wanted this fight almost, if not, more than Phil did.

"I wanna fight him," I croaked.

Brian shook his head as if he was shocked, "I'm sorry what? You, you wanna fight Phil, the son of Jupiter? You know, Jupiter. The big thunder dude from the Romans. He's like Zeus. Except a bit more ruthless."

I nodded my head. Gwen smirked as I did this. "We are gonna need to up your training Kyle. We need to prepare you for his tricks and tactics then." Gwen always had my back. Even when I acted like a jerk, she was always there for me. "Where do you want to start?"

Joey had walked over at this point, "Maybe his fighting tactics for one. Every time Phil goes into a fight he has a similar battle strategy. He gets his opponent tired and edgy, then he strikes with some lightning, and boom you're toast."

"Thanks Joey, that is really reassuring," I said sarcastically.

"Look kid," Joey began, which him beginning a sentence

36

like that was usually never good. "You need to figure yourself out. Who are you? What is your weapon? Figure out your questions and go from there."

I looked at him, "I am Kyle Pierce. My weapon of choice is a long sword named Shadow."

Joey went and grabbed a knife off of the wall. "Very well than Kyle. Draw your blade. Training time, and you are not skipping out of this one."

I drew Shadow and hefted it in my hand. The weight was a little top heavy, but it was my blade and I had grown accustomed to it. I swung it around and loosened my wrist and arms up.

"Good," Joey smirked. "Time to get down to some business then." He pushed a button on the wall and the room became a miniature Colosseum.

The twins sat in the stands drinking soda and holding popcorn. Either they were quick to attack the free food, or they had this planned. Gwen and Brian were no where to be seen though. The lighting grew dim as Joey stood in front of me wielding his knife.

"You get the first move kid," He said waving his arm for me to advance. I swung Shadow and was knocked aside by his knife. "Speed and agility will be your friends. Teddy Roosevelt may have talked about brandishing a larger stick than the opponent, but there is more to that." His voice trailed off as he walked into the shadow's. I blindly followed and swung where I thought he was.

Bad move!

His little 8-inch knife, parried my long sword and clattered it to the ground. I needed to get him, without questioning myself and my senses. I needed trust as well.

I heard a noise emit from the corner. I decided to advance towards it but not just rush in. I saw it was Joey with his back turned to me. I lifted up my blade to knock him down, and I myself was yanked to the ground instead.

As my head hit the floor I looked and saw a vine wrapped around both of my ankles. *Great! A trap.*

"Enemies love to lure you into a trap. You can either use it to your advantage or let it be your Achilles Heel." I could hear Gwen in the shadows as well. My best guess was Brian was also waiting there to teach me a lesson.

"How bout you come out and fight me Gwen. Quit hiding behind your plant powers."

Joey dimmed the lights even more. "Kyle, use your powers yourself. A fight won't be fair or even prove to allow any advantages if you do not try to reach your potential. Summon ice."

Joey was testing me. To not limit myself to my blade but use water in a combination. It wasn't a bad idea, except the ice part. The only thing I have practiced and still never able to actually do.

I closed my eyes and searched for any water. None that was spare, that is. I was able to sense Joey, and Gwen. I could feel the water within them flowing and I could trace their motions.

As I walked towards Gwen, a volley of arrows landed at my feet. "Fight against the odds," Brian said. Except Brian's voice was muffled. He had his mask on again.

I closed my eyes once I was in the center of the ring and listened to the water within Brian, Gwen, and Joey. They were surrounding me on the outskirts of the arena. Joey was not doing much but Gwen was summoning a fortress of vines and plants. Brian, *erh* Nightbow, lurked in the shadows having several arrows ready to take aim.

Use my advantage, I thought. Gwen's plants! Plant's need water to survive. That's how I could sense she was encasing the arena in plants. I focused on Shadow and struck its blade into the ground. The vines began to shrivel up and water dripped onto the dirt.

Perfect! Water for me to use and I had taken away Gwen's advantage. Brian's surprise factor was out the window as well. Now I just needed the speed and agility to take the three of them down.

Just then I realized I did in fact have a plan. If it was a good plan was a whole different question. I charged at Gwen. She shot out a vine at me, but I whistled once and got Brian to launch an arrow towards the sound of my whistle.

The arrow impaled the vine and allowed me to disarm the knife from Gwen. I slipped the blade into my pocket to use for later.

"Hey Brian," I shouted.

"It's Nightbow!" He yelled back.

At this point I had used him yelling to creep behind him. I held my blade like a baseball bat and said, "Yeah, I know." I raised the sword and hit him in the head with the blunt edge of the blade.

Joey slowly clapped in the center of the arena. "Well, done Kyle. You had a plan and used an advantage to outdo your opponent. You had a stealthy side, in an odd sense. But now, have you proven yourself enough to beat me?"

I walked to the center of the arena. Gwen had slowly begun to turn the lights back on. I hefted Shadow out in front of me, and readied my stance. "Tell me Kyle, can you win?"

"Yes!" I shouted as I launched myself at Joey. He eloquently fought back with his blade. It was like a small kid trying to pick a fight with another three times their height. Except this outcome ended with the smaller one coming out victorious. My blade clattered to the floor again.

I swiped the knife from my pocket slowly and raised my hands above my head, concealing the knife. Then I struck with a fierce speed. He read the attack, but it caught him off guard. He parried and deflected the blade. But it was too late. I gained the upper hand. In just under a minute I had disarmed him.

The others began to applaud. "Now you are ready kid."

CHAPTER 6

LET THE GAMES BEGIN

Thursday night was slow. We goofed off and played some video games. The twins built another seven building kits, and dozed off. None of us wanted to go to sleep in our rooms tonight.

As I fell asleep, and drifted into my dream, I was sitting on the beach in my dream. The waves crashed. I was in peace. The two children ran off in the distance playing tag. My usual dream.

I was half expecting another visit from the Inflictor, but no luck. I just sat by the seashore the whole night. An uneventful dream.

By morning I woke up and saw the bowl of chips and queso was empty. I got up, and went over to the elevator. Time to get my day started. My head felt heavy from the previous night. The sleep still hadn't left my eyes and I was sore from the training. I slowly trudged my way to the cafeteria and sat down at my seat.

I stared at my pancakes and began to pour syrup on them.

I yawned and the syrup began to overflow from my plate onto the table. Oh crap, I thought to myself.

"You slept in the bunker didn't you? You have zero preparation for tonight do you?" I looked over my shoulder and saw Hestia standing behind me.

"Lady Hestia, I, I uhm," I stammered.

"Cut the crap Pierce. I can't believe you're the one I'm supposed to be rooting for. What gift did I even bless you with when you were an infant?"

I scratched my head for a moment, "Quite frankly, I am unsure my Lady."

She shook her head, "That is right Kyle, I did not give you a blessing."

"Why is that?" Hestia was confusing me now, and it was definitely not helping that I was still groggy. I just wanted to eat some breakfast. Even though it was now almost lunch, so a brunch.

"Because Kyle," she began. Nothing ever got told to me positively like that. Chiron, Akhbar, Joey. Each and every one of them has said it to me at one point or another. "You lack motivation. You petty yourself to menial tasks. There are two quests to be administered by myself and Lady Hecate tonight. Each one has importance for a greater cause. Now you need to prove yourself worthy."

"*Psh*, c'mon Hestia, I don't need to worry. Myself and the

whole of Bunker 4921 are completely prepared for this."

"We shall see," she said walking away.

As it turns out we weren't. I went down to the Bunker an hour before the game and Gwen, and Brian were still evaluating the battle strategies.

I walked over to the table, "Uhm, what happened to my plan?" I thought they had liked it so I was confused as to why they were not using it.

Joey walked into the room, "Because it is not going to work tonight."

"Wha-but Joey," I said but was cut short by Gwen.

"We need you to stay back on defense with the twins watching over the other teams. The three of us will do recon in each zone with a select team from the other groups, and then we will strike. In addition, we want you away from Phil at all costs." That is where my frustration truly began to build.

"So I get the role of babysitting the trouble some duo?" I asked.

"Precisely!" Joey said handing me my blade. "Hecate and Hestia both have a quest to hand out. Two quests that Akhbar has approved. Now we just need one of them for our redemption."

Joey was focused. He really wanted to redeem himself and

the name of our Bunker after an incident we had caused a while ago.

We all made our way to the cafeteria and got into our groups. Chiron stood on a soap box, or tried to stand there. His four legs were presenting a bit of difficulty for him. "Team 1, report to the border now."

He was sending the teams out to the border to go to the Realm for the game.

We walked towards the border and were met with an open door. That usually does not happen. It's usually locked shut. I began to think; which Realm was it was it going to be? None of us knew for sure either. That is until we got there.

A city rose above us with skyscrapers painting the sky line. The grid like pattern of the street made the plan the other had come up with seem obsolete. There was no way they could pull off their spying mission on their own.

I knew what I needed to do now. Break the rules the Bunker gave me!

CHAPTER 7

I TASTE ELECTRICITY

I heard the alarm sound. The game was now beginning. I looked at Jim and Tim. "Hey guys, you're supposed to loose me in the field today, right?"

Jim cocked his head at me in confusion. Tim spoke up, "Uhm, that's exactly what we are not supposed to do according to Gwen."

I gave the boys a smirk and rubbed their hair. Their messy black hair was just a shaggy ball of fur, it seemed like. "Well, she isn't exactly in charge, is she?"

What I was doing was completely wrong. But just because Gwen thought I wasn't ready to stand my ground in battle, did not mean I had to necessarily listen to her. Brian was off scouting with Joey. Gwen was on the offensive. So, I could leave the twins to run defense alone here. Plus, it's not like I'd be purposefully looking only for Phil. I wanted to win the game for my team too.

I saluted the twins jokingly as I sprinted down the cityscape.

The streets were in a grid like pattern. Setting up optimal high points for archers to pick people off. I was about to be a prime target.

This realm was designed to rotate every time we came into it. This time it was about 4 square miles of a city. It was like a mix of major cities such as: New York City, San Francisco, Seattle, Washington D.C., Baltimore, and Miami. Which was a good mix for me because that meant it had water. Somewhere in here, it just meant I needed to find it.

Swords clashing brought me back to reality from my daze. I was near the center of the arena then. The Bonus Ball must've been ahead.

I could hear Joey's muttered war cries in the distance. This meant I should avoid going for the Bonus Ball.

I began to think of my bearings. If I was in the center I would need to decide which quadrant to enter. If we were the South, that left Phil and his Legionaries to be in either the West, North, or East. Good deducing Kyle, I thought to myself. The war cries began to near my location. I began to fear that I had been spotted.

I grasped my sword in my right hand and sprinted down the streets. I had to guess, and guess quickly on which way to go. RIGHT! My mind seemed to feel the urge to go that way. So naturally I chose to go left.

I dashed into the West quadrant and surveyed my surroundings. The buildings were lower here. The highest one was maybe reaching 10 stories high. This meant I was more open, more vulnerable to Phil's lightning as well.

I began to feel a surge in my gut. Water! I began to think pleasingly.

WHAM!

Out of nowhere a wall of water slammed into me. I staggered to pull myself up using my sword like a cane. My eyesight was dazed and I tried to snap out of it.

"My grammar may not be the best in the classroom, but I can still pack a punch in the battlefield," echoed the voice now towering above me. He swiped my leg out from under me, and my body fell to the earth like a sack of potatoes.

"Who in Hades are you?"

"My gods, how secluded are you down in that bunker Kyle? I'm Ethan Dorian, Son of Poseidon, and grandson of Hephaestus. The wielder of water and fire. We have a class together as well, jackass!"

I stood up and cracked my neck. Interesting he could control fire. A son of the sea could control fire. Come to think of it if I could control ice, maybe it wasn't impossible. But first I'd need to actually control ice.

Too late, I was thinking too much.

A ball of blue fire singed my eyebrows and burned my face.

I quickly retaliated by whipping a rope of water at my half-brother. In this process my blade had clinked against the floor. Ethan effortlessly grabbed my whip and lashed it back at me.

"Do not test me brother. I'm not just another training dummy like you Elite's got down in 4921."

This demigod, some legacy was equally as strong as me if not stronger. Why had I never challenged him before? I began to think how the past few days Chiron was pushing for me to use my ice abilities, as well as the rest of the Bunker. Maybe I could finally tap into them when I was in the face of danger.

I held out my hands pointing them at Ethan. I closed my eyes tight and tried to focus on just ice shooting out at him. My veins began to bulge in my forearms and sweat began to bead on my forehead.

"What in Odin's name do you think you are doing?"

I lowered my hands in disappointment. "I was really hoping my ice powers would work. I don't know. Now I look stupid. Alright hit me with your best shot."

I outstretched my hands waiting to get blasted by another ball of flames, when suddenly thunder rumbled throughout the street shattering the glass windows. "Pierce!"

I swear on Zeus' name, this son of Jupiter shot out at me like a bullet. As if he was lightning himself. His fist caught my back sending me tumbling into Ethan who helped to catch my fall. I found Phil, or well he found me it appeared.

"Two for one special I suppose? I'm earning my burger's tonight."

Ethan's hands lit up. He had stepped in front of me as if he was guarding me. Which was total bull, cause this kid wanted to fight me just as much as Phil Stryker did.

"Back off Sparky! This is my fight."

Phil felt the need to assert his dominance. Lightning began to spark up and down his arms as if snakes were wrapping around of him. The air began to smell a lot like rotten eggs, no wait, that was definitely sulfur. The clouds grew gray and ominous. Phil was preparing the perfect storm for his advantage.

I rolled myself to the sidewalk and had lifted up my sword. I frantically scanned the street's pavement in hopes of finding the water Ethan had hit me with. No such luck!

I began to think at the speed of a NASCAR car, there had to be something I could do. Why was I not witty like Brian? Then it hit me, all I needed to do was buy myself some time. At some point or another the groups would converge on this location.

"Hey you two. Why don't we just all go our separate ways and get the orbs for our quadrants. That way the game can go on. I mean Ethan isn't on defense are you?" I was hoping this would work. Ethan's eyes glimmered as if some of this was triggering a delay tactic. He was equally afraid of

Phil as myself. If I could spare us a fight with him, we might be in luck.

"No, I came here with the objective of securing the orb. I thought you were an enemy defender. So if we are all on offense we shouldn't be fighting then." Ethan's argument did not come across as strong as I was hoping. But as an advantage for me, I found a manhole cover. I know what you must be thinking, what on earth is he going to do with a manhole cover? Well, great question, cause I myself did not know yet.

"I do not care about you two, nor this game. What matters to me is defeating the two sons of Poseidon, who have ever so nicely been brought together. It must be fate. The legacy, and the child of the prophecy. Defeating you both together will make it so sweet and simple for the honor of Rome."

That's it, this guy needs to learn a little lesson. I readied my sword and flicked my sword at the son of Jupiter. My other hand focused on the manhole and it exploded.

Water surged around us. I had formed an arena and began to aid my enemy as well. He could electrocute the water and it'd fry Ethan and myself.

"So the child of the prophecy wishes to fight then?"

"It's not like I'm being given much of a choice here. Shall we call you Caesar as well?"

My mistake. Phil threw a bolt of lightning directly at

51

Ethan. It caught him square in the chest. He slumped to his knees slowly. Grasping his chest. The blast had fried his shirt to a crisp. His eyes had started to glaze over and then he hunched forward.

"One down. One to go."

I looked over as Ethan slowly moved. His movement was a desperate reach for the water. He reached towards a puddle. I slung some water in his direction in hopes he could heal himself.

Phil flipped his dice, Aureus, and it landed on a 1, a golden gladius sprung to life. Sword vs. Sword. Water vs. Lightning.

I rushed closer towards him, as he did likewise. Our swords met and sparks wicked off of his sword. After a few attacks and counters I had a misstep. My foot slipped on the wet pavement and Phil had the upper hand once again. He swung but my instincts took over. A wall of water splurged forward slapping him in the face.

"You insult disgrace of a fighter. You -"

I gave a halfhearted smirk, "Wow disgrace of a fighter? At least you got insult in there. Good vocabulary, Roman." I could see him growing increasingly irritated with me and my horrible witty comments.

Usually, I guess, if I had more time I could construct some awesome witty comment. When under pressure I must've looked like some fish out of water. Which no pun intended, I kind of was.

His fists charged with lightning. I knew at that moment I was a goner. "Oh balls," I muttered weakly.

"Kyle?" screamed a shocked voice down the road.

Phil rolled his eyes and dropped his arms in a frustrated manner, "Oh come on. What now? Can I not just zap you already? Do you mind if I get on with proving what a disgrace you are?"

"Uh, yeah I mind!" Yup that was my quick witted response. Probably not even worthy of me sharing with you guys. But you get the gist.

Phil raised his hands back up and sent a bolt of lightning into my left arm. I stumbled backwards and collapsed on the street.

"Kyle!" The voice was still audible in my mind. I heard some more lightning firing in the distance then my mind just went somewhere else.

***

I was a floating ghost again. I was standing in a room lit by four green torches. I was focused in on the girl in front of me. It was Vivian. That girl I saw in my dreams earlier in the week.

She had a cut on her forehead and a look of exhaustion and fear in her eyes. A voice came on the intercom demanding her to continue. It sounded very harmonious and robotic. A melodic tune filled the air. Hypnotizing.

Vivian stood back to her feet. Her knees were shaking. She flicked her arm forward and a bolt of electricity darted forward. A door appeared from where her bolt had struck.

The intercom voice rung out again. This time it said, "Progress to the next stage. Training is almost complete for the day."

I began to wonder what this training was for. But it more than likely had something to do with what had happened back at that convenience store. And I did not want any part of it.

***

My eyes began to flutter open. I was propped up in a bed in the infirmary section of the school. I wiggled my fingers on my left hand looking to see how badly damaged I was.

Funny, they had full motion.

I turned my head to my right and saw Brian and Gwen. Gwen had her head down sleeping. As Brian saw my head move he jolted forward and began to nudge Gwen to awaken her.

Brian pushed me back down as I tried to sit upwards. "No, you don't. Not so fast mister 'I can survive electricity.'" His voice had just a dash of sarcasm in it to annoy me.

"Wha-what happened after I got struck?" I managed to croak still tasting the sulfur in my throat, followed by a cough.

"What happened?" Gwen began to thunder. Ha, she thundered at me, and I got struck by lightning. Ha, anyone? Anybody? Oh yeah that's right. I'm writing this down. Whoops!

"You ruined the game! I was coming back to our zone with the last orb we needed , only to find you in a fight with Sparky! I had the game won Kyle, but you couldn't follow a simple order. Instead the twins were tied up. It's a miracle we didn't lose. You left Jim and Tim in charge of a group that is not even fit to brandish a stick!"

"That's a bit harsh," I retorted.

"A bit harsh there, really, am I the one in the wrong here Kyle? Jim is afraid of knives and barely uses his own sword!"

Brian sat back in his chair and began to scoot it farther and farther back. "If, uh, you two need some alone time, I think I might just slide on outta here."

Gwen turned her head and rolled her eyes at Brian. She had to have been thinking something along the lines of, are you flipping kidding me. Like can't you wait two minutes?

I didn't blame Brian. I wish I knew a way to get out of this one but I was stuck myself.

"Can't you just follow what we ask of you for once Kyle.

Stick to the books, it would help all of us out, a lot." Gwen's temper was beginning to flare, and it was nothing like I had ever seen before

I weakly shook my head, "I can't do that. That isn't me."

Just then Chiron had trotted into the room. He looked at Gwen and Brian, who was now scooting his chair around in circles in the back. "Kyle, I need to talk to you in private, immediately."

CHAPTER 8

I RELIVE MY PAST

"Chiron," Gwen began to plead. "Kyle didn't mean to harm that other son of Poseidon. He was using fire that was unfair and probably just startled him."

Sometimes I had really resented Gwen but other times I was glad she had my back. This time, yeah it was somewhere in between.

Startled, well a little. Since when does a child of Poseidon have flames curling in his hands. *Not normal. Nope!* To be honest, I don't even think I did anything in that fight. I didn't even get the chance to fight Ethan.

Chiron had seemed to be reading my mind, "Ethan is a legacy. His mother was the daughter of Hephaestus. He is technically a three-quarter blood. Three-fourths god, and well, one-fourth mortal. He somehow gets both Poseidon and Hephaestus powers. But you still had no right to engage him Kyle. And he is in one of your classes. Do you not pay attention?"

"I'm sorry Chiron. I really didn't think Phil would show

up and blast him. Plus, that was definitely not me that hurt him. You could look at the clothes Ethan was wearing and see the burn marks on his shirt."

Brian chuckled somewhere on the other side of the room, "He can't be that strong of a demigod if he gets blasted by lightning like that. Like, yikes!"

I perked my head up and just glared at Brian, "Not helping!" I lowered my gaze back to Chiron and saw his arms were now crossed.

"Bunker 4921 is supposed to be an elite group of demigods with each and every member there for a reason. They follow the rules on everything." When he had said everything it stung like a horde of wasps stinging me all at once. Long story short, yes that had happened to me. They say never to poke a hornet's nest, well add wasps to that list as well.

Ultimately, I deserved whatever punishment Chiron was ready to dish out upon me. Chiron had taken a deep breath. "So, congratulations on the win Bunker 4921, but I now do need to talk to Kyle in private. I will see you all at breakfast tomorrow morning. I'm sure Kyle will come consult you all in the Bunker later. Now Gwen, and Brian please report back to the Bunker immediately."

I watched as my friends walked away. Those two were true friends willing to try to help me get out of trouble.

I closed my eyes and heaved myself up in the bed. "So what else is actually up Chiron. I know you as well now,

Chiron, and that was not why you wanted to talk. You've been privately training me for years incase you forgot, so I know you as well now."

Chiron lowered his gaze, "You know that I strongly believe you are a child of the prophecy, if not the main child. I believe you are him. Well, each child of this prophecy has what the gods call a mentor. A god or goddess that is not their parent who will give them advice, assistance, or even help when going on a quest and well it is time for your first quest."

I paused, "A...a quest? Like actually have some point other than eradicating some small village of some monster?"

"Precisely, of sorts. So before you embark on it, you must go and consult your mentor. Out of our games three guests: Mars, Hecate, and Hestia. Lady Hecate watched your performance at the game and has tasked you to consult your mentor and embark on this quest of hers which your mentor knows about."

I eagerly perked up, forgetting each and every drop of pain welting in my arm. "Well, who is my mentor? What is my quest?"

Chiron smirked and laughed, as if I was about to be let in on a huge secret. "Your mentor is none other than the god of Tricksters, and he will guide you for your quest."

"Hermes?" I asked in confusion.

"Gods no!" Chiron snorted holding back a laugh. "Your father chose your mentor to be none other than Loki!"

My face sunk immediately and I had wished I had gotten anyone other than Loki. Bunker 4921 had an encounter with the Norse god of tricksters a few years ago when I was only 11.

***

We were in the middle of Kansas trying to take down the Karkadann, a shadowy rhino-like monster. Really big and menacing. It was pretty much just one giant klutz. Usually it's smart and stays in its homelands out of sight and out of mind. However, it was taking down farm houses and we needed to attempt to extract it from the area before it would do more damage.

It had begun to put up too much of a fight and had attacked some statue as Brian tightened its reigns. The Karkadann slammed Brian into the statue and out of nowhere a sudden burst of flames erupted from the statue.

Before us now, stood a slender man in gold plated armor and a long black hair. He smirked slyly and said, "No one messes with a statue made in my honor. NOBODY and NOTHING!" And with that he unleashed one of the most violent attacks that poor Karkadann had probably ever seen. The monster fell to its side as Loki sized up the members of Bunker 4921. "You demigods dare let this one horned monster touch my statue."

"Uhm, we are sorry sir but I didn't know this statue belonged to you," Joey had said trying to smooth over the situation.

"*Pft.* Demigods. I should have figured when I heard the commotion. I should have let you all perished instead. They say the hide of one of these Persian beasts is very valuable but that it also attracts other monsters as well. I bid you all luck."

He disappeared in a tuft of flames and left nothing except a dead Karkadann. He then shortly returned behind Gwen and followed her shadow and emerged from it. He stood there for a second and then shouted "BOO!" Gwen nearly had a heart attack as Loki just sat there laughing. He was almost at the point of rolling on the floor he laughed so hard.

He then stood up and slicked his hair back again. "Now demigods, I recall being informed that you are the elite of your kind. That you will face much worse than this in due time. Like my pet here. I will leave you to fight him."

"Wait, what?" I asked in confusion.

Too late. Loki had already left and we couldn't find the pet he left us. I doubted that he left us anything at all. Other than trickery of course. We searched for at least an hour around the small town afraid something was lurking and just waiting to kill us or harm the civilians. No such luck. Instead it was like someone had gone to the mall with three pigs and labeled them: 1, 2, and 4. Just to send the security guards on a wild goose chase. Well, yeah, that idea was probably invented by none other than Loki himself.

We walked around and after several hours finally decided to leave the town. Loki didn't actually leave anything, or if he did we were just really bad at hunting for it.

***

Over my years at Demigod Central I had met many gods, but never Loki. At least not at Demigod Central. Loki, I had met only once on the battlefield. And well, from what I knew of him personally, I didn't like him. And I would most certainly not enjoy meeting him at his home where he was truly in control.

CHAPTER 9

THE SON OF JUPITER

"What do you mean, Loki is my mentor? Chiron he is not one that I want on my side. Can't I just pick who I want as my mentor? Someone who can maybe teach me a new ability or something at all? But Loki isn't he just going to trick me and be vague?" I waited for Chiron to tell me anything, but he sat there with a puzzled look upon his face.

"Your father picked Loki because he trusted he would help you in the long run. Do not underestimate Loki either. He is a powerful god in the Norse culture."

I got out of the bed and stamped my foot against the ground in frustration. I began to walk back to the dorms ticked off beyond belief. Chiron called out, "Kyle, be mindful and keep a cool head. Do not let Loki being your mentor get to you in a bad manner. Do not let Loki see frustration either, or he will go to town messing with your mind."

"Thanks Chiron," I sarcastically said in frustration as I turned and walked away in anger.

I walked past Headmaster Akhbar's office and noticed he was out again.

Our Headmaster was gone every other day it seemed. He was always off doing his own thing and never there for us. Except when he wanted to yell at us for doing something wrong.

As I continued walking down the hall, I saw the door labeled, *DO NOT ENTER, LARGE SNAKE INSIDE.* I had noticed it was a new sign. Maybe it had a new resident inside. Used to be something Chiron called, El Chupacabra. But heck if it was the real thing that would've impressed me. Instead now we had got some snake. Eh, not really important I guessed.

I walked out to the glass bridge and stared out in the distance. Out on the purple horizon I stared at the clouds. The skyline was always magnificent at Demigod Central. It wasn't tied to the rules of the solar system that Earth rotated in. Although I did appreciate the fact we did still cycle on the 24-hour time table.

I felt the air pressure drop as another demigod stood next to me. Mimicking my stance, leaning against the railing peering off into the distance. My eyes glanced to the side. I noticed his blonde hair and striking blue eyes, Phil Stryker.

"Congrats on the win. I presume Chiron gave you a quest as well? Who sanctioned your quest, Mars as well?"

Phil had never been the one to flat out congratulate me, so

this was new. A little too new and different for my taste. I guess he has caught me off guard. "Yeah, I first get to go consult my Mentor. And no not Mars, Hecate did."

"Ah, so you are accepting this quest than? Hecate is always an odd choice to offer a quest. Sounds more like she needs you to clean something up for her."

Clean something up for her. Did Phil know of my dream with the Inflictor and Hecate's daughter? I looked at Phil cross eyed. "What do you know about this quest?"

He snickered at me. I was still unsure if I could trust this son of Jupiter or if he was trying to get into my mind. "Listen here Kyle, I've got my own mission to attain to. You will probably do well in your quest."

"What mission?"

"Besides the point. My mission, my business. Anyway, I'm wishing you luck out in the real world. Chiron may train you here, but out in the real world it is a lot more intense. No one is gonna walk by and hold your hand. Loki won't come and just aid you again, like he did in Kansas."

"I'm not asking anyone to hold my hand Phil! Especially Loki!" He had found the short fuse on me and was ready to light it.

"Ha, you act as if you are a Roman at times, but for a majority of the time we see your true graecus colors, Kyle. Wild and unpredictable. Sparta may have embraced you with open arms, but not I."

"What's your mission anyways?"

"To acquire the Ancile of course. I know where it is, how many guards are there, and everything. It'll be a quick snatch and grab Kyle, unlike the garbage they have you picking up. A book from Minerva's collection. How important." The sarcasm rolled out of his mouth as though it was second nature.

Phil began to walk away but I began to wonder what he was talking about. I turned and tossed my sword, Shadow, through his purple cloak. "Wait!"

"Some nerve you have son of the sea. You must feel like a hot shot now don't you. Just because you're team won a game, by a crazy forfeit rule, does not mean you are invincible now." I saw Phil's hands begin to charge with electricity. His blue eyes throwing sparks everywhere. I swallowed a hard lump in my throat. Phil tossed my sword aside and marched away. As he walked further down the glass bridge I heard him say, "Going after that book is a suicide mission anyways kiddo. It may all just be a giant trap set by Akhbar himself."

I picked up Shadow and slung it back into my backpack. I squinted my eyes at the Roman and then towards the dorms. I needed to get back to the Bunker right away. I needed to inform the others we would be visiting Asgard very soon. Well, more like Loki's palace, but they wouldn't go if I told them who we were going to see.

The thought of me being some big shot hero scared me a bit. I knew I was destined to be one, yet it was only an idea to ever cross my mind for a second. That I could be a legend like Achilles, Odysseus, Aeneas, Hercules, Jason, and all the others kept scaring me. But if it was something I needed to do, I needed to start acting like I was one.

CHAPTER 10

WE MEET LOKI... A.K.A. THE GOD OF ANNOYANCE

Chiron had decided it was best we left at dawn. So that meant no late night weekend revelries in the Bunker. However, knowing what was in store for the morning, I decided to heed Chiron's advice and try to get some sleep. Unfortunately, I fell asleep instead of staying up and watch Brian sharpening his arrows under his desk lamp.

My dream was peculiar. I was sitting on a beach as waves crashed at my feet. Children laughing was heard in the distance. A boy and a girl. Their voices echoed in my dream. They laughed and began to taunt me. "The boy who lost everything to gain nothing." They said this over and over again. And with each word the sky grew darker and storms began to plague the beach.

The boy walked forward. He looked similar to me except for his eyes. They were pitch black. With each step he took the ground shook and miniature earthquakes rippled out. "You expect to be a hero when you are nothing. You don't even know where to begin! Your quest will fail"

Behind me the girl made her advances bringing with her a storm of swirling winds, a hurricane. The hurricane flicked around her hand as she was just twirling a finger. "You fail to realize what potential lies in you! Your heart is cold, yet can't produce ice."

Each word she spoke was a wind ripping out of her lungs, and slapping me in the face, berating me with each syllable. "Your father has taught you nothing and everything you know is different then what it should be. You know so little of the world. Can you even trust your friends in the end?"

My body began to feel cold. As the two got closer and closer I felt my body turn to ice. Once they placed their hands on my shoulders I shattered to pieces and woke with a start.

I sat upright and my body was shaking. *Ok,* I thought to myself. *Creepy twins are creepy. Check!*

***

The next day I did not want to talk much at breakfast. I sat idle at the table as Joey was giving everyone instructions on how to act, mainly the twins and Brian. However, my mind was elsewhere. These twins, that oddly resemble me, just made me question everything. Why do I have to get information from Loki, instead of my own father.

Anger began to fill my veins until Chiron hoof clanked into the table, and I came back to reality.

"Isn't that enough syrup for your pancakes Kyle?"

"Wha-WOAH!" I nearly jumped out of my seat as syrup began to flood off the table to the floor. "I - I uh-dozed off."

Chiron looked at me as if his telepathic powers were at work once more. Did centaurs have telekinesis? Who knows. I thought they were just half-horse, half-man, or woman. I insulted a female centaur once. Didn't go so well. In my defense she had some very masculine features.

He continued to talk, "Are you all prepared to meet with Loki today?"

Brian's fist slammed on the table, "Dammit, Loki! Are you kidding me? I wanted to talk with Thor, or Odin. But we get this stuck up-"

"Brian!" Joey interjected to try to get his attention. "So we need to have a meeting with Loki? This is who Kyle's mentor is? The jerk that had us running circles in the middle of nowhere Kansas?"

Chiron made a worried smile, "Uhm-well precisely. He is after all who Poseidon chose to watch out for his son."

Gwen rolled her eyes. The twins looked at everyone, "So we get to go to Asgard and meet Loki. AWESOME!"

***

The portals drained us as always. But we arrived in Asgard. I had been here only once before, and it was for some field trip. Yikes, it was a crazy trip. Ha, like I remember when this, erh. I'm getting sidetracked again. I'll back down and get back on track.

We walked through Asgard as if we were little kids in a toy store. Everything fascinated us. The weapons, the smells, the food. All of it was so very different from Olympus. Even the clothing.

Brian looked at several guys passing and saw them wearing hooded cloaks. "I want one."

Joey squinted and looked at him, "I'd call you a Dork in a Hood."

"I don't care Joey. Do you know how kick ass that'd be? Just walking down the street and seeing a Native American archer with a hood attack."

Gwen couldn't control herself from laughing. "I'd think they'd laugh before they'd cower. Don't you already have a mask, and a jacket?"

"I'm getting one to complete my ensemble. Nightbow lives on!"

Brian marched into a store buying a cloak for himself. He came out wearing it with a look of satisfaction across his face. Joey and Gwen began to make a bet how long it would take for Loki to laugh at him. Personally I didn't think it would take that long at all for people to laugh.

Loki's palace was a cold and desolate place on the

outskirts of Asgard. Not much was left in it. It actually looked like it had been abandoned for a long time.

Cobwebs were strewn in the corners as Joey lit a torch we could hear the smoldering and crackling of several spiders nested within. A faded portrait of Loki hung over a mantle as a fire burned low within it. It burned slowly and gave off a cold chill to the room.

I stared into the fireplace as I saw flames depicted a scene of a boy falling into a pit while impaling a knife into his attempted rescuer. A voice that sent a chill through my body spoke softly, "So it is a shame that the fire showed you a vision, did it not?"

"I'm sorry what?" I said startled and turned to see the god in front of me, Loki god of tricksters and fire.

His hair was black and looked like silk as it fell across his back. He wore a green hooded cloak with the hood down and had gold platted armor on his chest, wrists, and lower legs. He smirked as I looked at him, "Why hello there young half-blood. You seek your future do you not?"

Joey tightened his gaze as he sized Loki up, "Aren't you the Norse god of tricksters and fire, not futures?"

Loki's smile faded as he turned to pace around Joey, "Ah the son of the Sun! What an honor it is. And might I ask about your decision?" Joey staggered backwards and in some confusion. "Of course I know about that Mr. Schmitz. I know all your endeavors, and how should I put it, side tasks."

As I looked at Joey I noticed his fists were clenching. Something Loki was saying was getting at him. It was as if Loki was taking personal jams at him.

Loki smiled again as he motioned towards Gwen. "Ah, Gwen Mahoney! My, my. I'm looking at a great leader and Daughter of Demeter!" Loki kneeled and kissed her hand. "My honor to be in your presence." She pulled her hand back and held it awkwardly as Loki had stood up. "Your fate is interesting. Freyr must've had a hand in your fate. Also your role as leader of Bunker 4921." Loki eyed Joey and said, "Too soon?"

Brian had been in a staring contest with the god since he had gotten there. "And as I make my rounds, the younger Schmitz, Brian, is it?"

Brian had finally blinked, "Why yes it is, Brian Schmitz at your service!"

Loki smiled, "I like this child, why can't you all be like him. I demand all demigods be more like him. And more fashionable as well. Nice cloak."

Joey, Gwen, and my own jaw dropped as Loki had said that. Brian took the complement and bowed politely. "Why thank you Lord Loki."

I nudged Brian and looked at Loki as he sat on a throne of fire. He wasn't exactly sitting in it as much as he was

lounged about it. His legs were thrown over one of the arms
as he threw his head back against the other. "So what really
brings you here? You did not wish to see the beginning of
Ragnarök, Kyle Parker, so why are you here?"

"Parker? It's Kyle Pierce." I said with a snap. Although
even my confidence on my last name was weak. "Anyways I
was sent here by Chiron, trainer of Greek heroes, erh all
heroes, to seek your advice. I am the son of Poseidon and
need some advice about you being my mentor."

"Your mentor," he retorted sitting up properly in his
throne. "Why this makes this encounter much more
interesting." He paused and placed his hands on his chin
and elbows on his knees. "Welcome to Asgard! I will do my
worst to advise you."

Joey pushed forward towards Loki's throne of fire. "What
do you mean by your worst, Loki? Are you not supposed to
be helping us defeat this threat?"

"Listen boy, in due time I will assist in the demise of the
enemy. But for now it is best you concern yourself what lies
in the eminent future." He paused and looked around a bit
distracted. "It is only you here, correct? Like Thor is not
near is he?"

"Uh, no? It is only us, why?"

He nervously peered around the room a bit anxious, "You
are sure, correct? Last time I saw my 'brother' I had given
him an insult greater than any regarding his wife, Sif."

"Brother? In air quotes?" I asked a bit confused, "Aren't you brothers in those Marvel movies?"

He rolled his eyes, "Creative differences and what not, but anyways back to-"

Gwen stared at him recalling the story and had cut Loki off, "Thor chained you to a rock and had poison drip into your eyes. How did you escape?"

Loki rolled his eyes, "Does it matter how I escaped? The past is in the past. Yet, my eyes suffered enough but not enough for me to still be undoubtedly wise. Now do you wish to know your task?"

"Yes," I said without hesitation. I felt like it was rude but I meant it. The more time I had spent with Loki the more annoyed I was getting. My temper was beginning to flare with each thing he said.

"My oh my, you are pushy, are you not? Maybe your father was right, maybe you aren't the one. Well, this will be interesting to see how everything unfolds."

"What do you mean me not being the one?"

"You have not yet heard the prophecy. Which is best. Wait two years, then decide your fate. I gave you a glimpse into the future through the fire, learn it. But for now, I need you all to travel to the new world's capital, Washington D.C., find the know-it-all, secure the book, and return to Demigod Central. If you succeed you succeed, which is good. If failure is what you achieve, then it is the end for one of you. Have fun figuring it out. And good luck in D.C., tourists this time of year are very pushy and rude. Who knows, maybe there's a helpful one in the bunch. Oh and also, only three of you can embark on this quest in order to get to your location and succeed."

We looked at one another, and Brian finally spoke up, "Sounds like a riddle. Can we get more of a prophecy?"

Loki slumped his shoulders, "Ugh, fine. Half-Blood's and your pesky vague futures. Very well," his eyes began to glow white and a voice spoke throughout the hall echoing.

The journey of three shall begin by sea.

For one they must face their past,

Another a sacrifice must be made,

And the third, will stand alone in the end.

For if more than three embark,

they will not make it out together.

Brian furrowed his brow, "I liked the first one better. Can you try rewording it Loki?"

Loki's eye's reverted back to normal, "I like your style boy but do not test your luck. You wanted a prophecy well, you got something like one. I am not like Apollo's accursed Oracle of Delphi. If I knew it were up for grabs I would have stopped that kid from ever getting his hands on such a spirit."

Gwen spoke up once more, "Didn't Apollo come into existence before you and the Nordic people though?"

"Aside from the point. Just, don't worry about it. You have received a prophecy of sorts. So back to your school and do not speak of me being free of my captivity."

***

We walked back through Asgard more flustered than before. On the plus side we found out where the book in question was. So I guess we learned something out of all of Loki's lunatics.

As I thought on what he had said, me not knowing the prophecy, and my dad's doubts. How could he not trust me? He barely knew me. I realized then that I had to accomplish this quest with success in order to try to impress my dad.

CHAPTER 11

I MAKE A PAINFUL CHOICE

As we walked back through the portal and into Demigod Central, I couldn't shake Loki's terms. Only allowing three to go on this quest left me with a knot in my stomach. This was going to be a rough choice for me to make.

I couldn't take Jim or Tim. That was a given for an obvious reason. If I took those two, I'd be on a constant babysitting journey instead of searching for this book.

I had to choose to leave Gwen, Brian, or Joey behind.

Ultimately, I had to choose to leave Gwen behind. It was one of the toughest decisions I ever had to make.

My reasoning was this, Joey had experience in the real world, so he was an obvious. And quite frankly when it came down to it, Brian was my best friend. So I had to pick him. Plus, I did not know much about D.C. so I wasn't sure if taking an archer-swordsman, or an arborkinesis was the better choice. I had heard it was a city so I figured there was not an abundance of plants around it.

I pulled Gwen aside when we were alone later that evening in the Bunker. And, well, I told her my choice. I could see the pain welling up in her eyes. I had hurt her in the way that I had told her.

I tried to walk up to give her a hug and tried to apologize. Instead her reaction was fierce.

"Back off Kyle!" she shoved my backwards and a few vines began to sprout at my feet.

"This is a bit of an over reaction Gwen."

"You of all people know how badly I wanted to go through the Realms and go to visit Washington! Could you not just let me have that satisfaction?"

I rolled my eyes at her. "Gwen, this is serious-"

She had cut me off to begin her own, "Oh serious? You mean to go find some book?"

"Well, yeah. And since when did you want to visit Washington?"

"Have fun then Kyle. You somehow managed to push even me over the edge. And to think that I-" Gwen froze in fear. She spun around after clutching her mouth and marched away.

I had just realized why Gwen was so upset. I should have done something different. Maybe I could persuade Chiron to let me take a fourth. But alas, I knew Chiron wouldn't permit such a peril without having one of us stay. That way in case all hell broke loose, there would always be one of us to take over as leader.

I was a bit shaky. Gwen had never been this upset with me before. In the past it had all been just fun and games, when we would joke around. But I knew she wanted to get out of Demigod Central, but I did not want her in harms way. "Gwen, I'm sorry. I was trying to protect you."

She paused and looked angrily upon me. The silence was so loud. It was painful to hear it, or to hear nothing. Gwen began to storm out and she stopped at the doorway. "What were you even trying to protect me from Kyle?"

I had to pause to think of how it would be best to word this. "Gwen-" my voice broke. I couldn't do this. Not now at least. I couldn't take her on the quest. And I couldn't admit that I might be starting to have feelings for her. I needed to keep this friendship plutonic.

"That is what I thought Kyle. You are rash like the sea, and your heart is cold much like the ocean's depths. This is why you won't make a good leader one day with this prophecy. You fail to relate to us. You are self-centered. And dare I say it a lot like Narcissus."

I couldn't move for two reasons. One, my feet were tied up. And well two, I was speechless. But what she had said, what had she said again? I looked like Narcissus, well with that I wouldn't complain, but no that could not be it. She must have been mad that I did not pick her, and that I was trying to be the good guy and keep her safe. *Whoops*, guess that wasn't my place.

Well, as she walked away I realized I had just ruined every shot I had at being more then friends after this was all done. As the elevator dinged I realized she was going to leave me here with the vines engulfing my feet.

"Hey, uh, Gwen!" I began to shout. "Can you help me with the vines?"

She shouted back, "Why don't you get your quest mates to help!"

Did she just have a bit of British in her voice?

Anyways, back to me being stuck with vines around my feet.

Jim came over to me and began to laugh. "You know, if you had practiced more maybe you could summon ice out of the water moisture in the air."

I looked at him half ready to strangle him, "Yea, well if I had time I may have, but instead I'm kind of tied up. Care to pass me a knife?"

He shook his head frantically like I had just asked him to kill someone. "Only Tim can use knives. I always screw up and, nope sorry." He ran off like a scared puppy with its tail between its legs. Great there goes my help for the night.

I sat contemplating what Jim had told me, that if I had

practiced more, maybe, just maybe I could summon ice. Although then again, I realized I was pretty lazy, so yeah. I did not want to practice, but I figured I would give it another shot here.

I closed my eyes and concentrated on the moisture in the air. I picked up on them, little particles floating in the air. They began to come together and form a knife. When I went to go pick it up, it splashed to the ground as little drops of water.

"Dammit-" I slammed my fist at thin air and then I opened my eyes and the knife was at my feet. "What?"

"I placed it there while your eyes were closed," Tim said from the corner. "You've really done a number on Gwen this time Kyle. You know she's been developing a crush on you recently. But you just seem like one of Jim and my machine's. Pretty dang heartless."

I looked at him as I cut through the vines. "You know, for being so young, how in Hades name are you so smart? And have you been here the whole time even when Jim ran off?"

"Whole time, and I blame Hephaestus," he said shrugging his shoulders. "So Gwen is getting left to be our babysitter?"

I nodded. "I can't leave Brian here, or he would need a babysitter too."

"That's a good point," he said calmly.

"Thanks for the knife. I'll see you later bud." I began to

walk towards the elevator, waiting to go back to my room, and escape this torture I was bringing to myself.

My ID beeped against the elevator scanner as my badge was accepted.

I trudged back to my room, and saw Brian adding gold stitches to his newly acquired hood. I slumped down on my bed and held a photo of Gwen, and myself as I laid in bed.

Brian's sewing machine hummed away. As he finished the last little bit he turned the machine off and looked at me, "So I heard you picked who's going. Although I already knew who you'd pick."

I put the picture down and looked at him with his magnifying glasses on. "You realize that Gwen's liked you for a few weeks now?"

"Yes!" I agonizingly croaked out while slumping my face into my pillow. "I realize I was extremely stupid here, and she is gonna hate me now."

"Well, to be blunt, you were a dumb ass!"

"What the hell Brian?"

"You had a girl you liked, who liked you back, but were to much of a dummy not to act on it! You are a first class dummy."

I grew irritated and said through my gritted teeth, "Take it back."

"Make me!" Brian jeered.

So from there I attacked Brian like a pouncing jungle cat. His scream woke our neighbors, and when they came to the door we reluctantly answered.

Larry stood at the door with a serious case of acne and bed head. We both cringed a bit seeing him at the door. His eyes were squinted trying to keep out the light. Larry was a son of Hypnos, but we gave him the nickname of Larry the Lazy since he never did anything but sleep.

"You all are causing a ruckus!" He had put such an emphasis on ruckus that me and Brian couldn't help but let out a giggle. His eyes got even squintier than they already were. "Do not make me complain to the hall spirits."

"C'mon Larry, we both know the spirits of the hall are just a tale we tell the kids to keep them scared at night."

A slight smirk crept across Larry's face, "Tell that to Deborah then. The wailing spirit of our hall."

"Deborah isn't real. C'mon man think logically," I said amused. Brian still couldn't help himself from laughing.

"DEBORAH!" Larry began to shout.

Brian was in an uncontrollable laughter, "Calm down Raymond."

Just then a wailing voice spoke out, "Who's causing a disturbance?"

The shade appeared a few doors down as Larry pointed into our room. "Holy moly! She's real!" My jaw was nearly on the floor.

Brian kicked the door and latched all three locks on the door. He frantically sprinted backyards and crawled to his bow. He notched an arrow in it and aimed it at the door. "Deborah is real?!?" Brian was so jittery he looked like he had just drank about five espresso's.

After Larry's door closed I began to crack up. "Oh my gods Brian. Did you see yourself. Did you crap your pants while you were at it?"

"No," he quickly checked himself really quickly. "Yeah, no I didn't. But Deborah. That creepy ghost is real. How on this Realm am I going to sleep tonight?"

"One, put your head on your pillow and close your eyes. And secondly did you really just say, 'how on this Realm?' Like who says that?"

"I just did. We aren't on a world, or Earth. We are on a floating island in the middle of nowhere dimension!"

I shrugged my shoulders he had a point. But on the plus side, Larry had settled Brian and me from fighting more with one another. I should send him a fruit basket. Or some acne cream. Like he would like that, right?

CHAPTER 12

THE KNIGHT AND THE WITCH

Well, if the thought of a wailing spirit named Deborah wasn't enough to give you a nightmare then I don't know what would. Well for me, drowning, but that's a story for another time. Now I know what you are thinking, my fear is drowning, well yes, but that was a while ago, and there is a reason I don't train much nowadays.

Now I was laying in my bed sitting and thinking. Wondering if this quest was even worth it. Phil was sent out to retrieve an Ancile. Which was like a great treasure hunt. Whereas my task seemed like an errand. And why was Hecate the one administering this quest for Athena? Why didn't we get a prophecy from her? Why was this book so important to Hecate?

Funny thing is, when you fall asleep, dreams latch onto your thoughts as you slip into the unconscious.

I opened my eyes and looked out at the beach once more. My sanctuary. The boy and girl played off in the distance as they always had. The sea air filled my lungs. Each wave lapsing over the previous as it crashed to the shore. I had filled my hand with sand and let it pour out before me.

As the sand was seeping through my fingers an image began to flicker in place of the beach and the kids. I was in a warehouse building watching a man with weathered skin in gold-plated armor attack a training dummy with a golden sword. Whoever this guy was, I think it was a safe bet to guess his favorite color was gold.

I sat on top of a shelf watching his strikes and blows to the dummy, until the dummy spilled all the sand at once with one fatal strike. His fighting tactics were fluent and each of his movements was graceful and perfect.

He sighed and then recovering his breath blurted out, "Another!"

A girl came into view, in her hands was a large leather bound book. No way, I began to think to myself. The girl was Vivian, and in her hands was the Book of Shadows.

She flicked her wrist and the sand fixed itself back into the training dummy. The swordsman in the gold knight armor smiled. "Thank you, girl."

"The name is Vivian, and I still do not understand why I am your partner for this mission."

The golden knight practiced another move and swiftly decapitated the training dummy like it was butter. He turned towards Vivian and his smile was wicked.

I slowly began to climb down the shelf and scale to another to get a better vantage point.

"Look, Vivian, the Inflictor granted you the power to hold the book because you are a daughter of Hecate, the only true witch to wield the book's true potential. If I were to speak or even try to read the mumbo jumbo of that book it would do nothing. Plus, you will plant the book for them to find. I wish to test my brother and see how this prophecy will play out in the future."

"So this is all a game to you?" Vivian aggressively said.

The golden knight smirked again laughing to himself. "Oh this is rich girl. Or *sorry*, Vivian. You do know who I am right?"

Vivian snarled, "Yes, you are the Golden One. The brother of Pegasus."

The Golden One as Vivian had called him hefted his gold blade and held it to Vivian's throat. "If I was not ordered to protect you, and carry out this mission, I would treat you like any other demigod I have met. Mount your head with the numerous collection I have gathered through the ages. My mother was killed by a son of Zeus, and from her blood I was born. I want nothing but to be the best and stop any demigod in my way. So the fact the Legion has me babysitting is just a giant joke. They are laughing at me! I sit on the Council and they are mocking me as we speak."

Vivian pushed the sword away from her throat. "Fine!

We shall do it your way boss. But where has the Inflictor gone off to if he is not overseeing our mission."

"The Legion's higher up's are upset he gave you the spell to save the life of Hector Tribe. A prophet of ours has spoken of his future to the Council of Tartarus and they decided on his death instead. Anyone who accompanies him will face death."

Vivian lowered her head. She obviously still had some sort of feelings for this Hector kid. I began to wonder if it was worth looking for this kid myself. Maybe it was a better quest then Hecate's little errand she's assigned.

"The snakes seek interest in him for some reason. Do you know why Vivian?"

"We had a run in with some serpent creature a few months ago. Hector killed it and now snakes have been after him ever since."

"I wish I could hunt the Inflictor's mistake and kill this fallen hero myself. And by the way some clean up crew got to it first before we could retrieve it. That snake was important to us."

"We have a task to do Chrysaor. Let's get back to it."

Vivian waved her hand and the warehouse went dark. Chrysaor and Vivian were gone. And I began to have the feeling that they would be waiting for our arrival in D.C. now.

The two kids were staring at me now. I was back on the beach and somehow drew attention to myself. They began to sprint towards me in a slow then a rapid change of pace. I tried to stand up, but instead the sand was swallowing me more and more as I struggled. Quicksand? No it was beach sand. This was just a dream. The image of Chrysaor slicing the sand dummy's head off flashed through my eyes. The blade connecting with the dummy stuck. His blade had done that to other demigods, and demigods were not some sand filled object.

The twins were closing in on me with blinding speed. They quickly shifted forms and were now the wailing spirit of Deborah. As I screamed with fear she had slashed through what was left of my body as it was swallowed by the sand.

I sat upright in bed with a start. A cold sweat was beading down my face. I looked at my alarm clock and saw it was 6:50 AM. Somehow our dimensional island still followed the 24-hour time cycle of Earth fairly well.

Brian was still fast asleep. He was cuddling with his bow and had a spare quiver loaded with arrows at his bed side. He was definitely one person that I did not want to startle when they were in a deep sleep.

I laid my head back onto the pillow. I really needed to stop thinking before I fell asleep and just fall asleep and let my mind wander instead of focusing on it.

CHAPTER 13

A NEW GIRL IN THE 4921

BZZT! BZZT! BZZT! BZZT! BZZT!

My alarm began to spaz out on top of my nightstand. I sat up in my bed and began to rub the sleep out of my eyes. As I reached over to turn it off I noticed it had said 8:05 AM.

A split second before my hand hit the snooze button an arrow impaled my alarm clock and pinned it against the wall. "The f-"

"Why are you waking me up early!" Brian sounded pretty ticked off. The scary thing was his eyes were still shut, yet had still managed to get a perfect shot at my alarm clock.

"You're lucky my hand wasn't there!"

Brian sat up groggily and didn't raise his head yet as he yawned and spoke, "I don't miss. That's also cause I don't decide my target always before I fire my arrow."

"What?! Like that is dangerous and not at all safe."

"Safety is what those warning labels are for. I, my friend,

am a human being. I don't have any warning labels on me. So by default I can be me."

I scratched my head then stretched. I looked at the floor and noticed my backpack was already packed. Shadow, my two-handed long sword leaned against the wall. A note rested on my bag,

Meeting with Headmaster at noon. Be prompt!

~Joey

I walked over to Brian and showed the note to Brian. "When did he get into our room?" Brian was freaking out. "No, no, no. My cloak is gone!"

"The one from Asgard?"

"Yea," he sounded bummed out. "The one Loki thought was cool. Dang!"

Secretly I had hidden his cloak. It was bad enough he had the mask and the jacket, we did not need to keep encouraging this Nightbow fantasy he had.

I slipped into my jeans and laced up my sneakers. Threw a red t-shirt on and then found one of Brian's t-shirt hoodies that he had outgrown. I quickly brushed my hair and then brushed my teeth.

I looked over at Brian as he finishing tying his boots. He slipped on his leather jacket and pushed his balaclava into his jacket's pocket. He slung a quiver over his back and tossed a few others into my magic backpack. Time to go to breakfast.

As we walked through the mess hall, half-bloods turned and whispered to the others as we walked by. Probably pointing out how stupid our quest was, or Brian's jacket. I wanted to say it was probably his jacket, but it was most likely our quest.

I sat down at the table with the rest of the Bunker. Minus a Gwen Mahoney. Jim looked at me like I was a stranger, "Gwen's pissed at you Kyle."

I rolled my eyes and sarcastically said, "Tell me something I don't know."

"Ok, how about, we are getting a new member in the Bunker!" Tim said with one of those stupid smiles that just make you want to knock it off of their face.

My eyes darted quickly. Usually an addition had to be decided by a trial, how could Akhbar, Chiron, and Joey break tradition for this person? Plus, we had not had a member join since the twins. Jim and Tim were too excited about this. And why did Gwen get to do the introductions? All of us were present at breakfast minus the daughter of Demeter.

I looked at my plate of waffles and decided I was not as hungry as I thought I was. I finished my orange juice and sausage, and grabbed my bag. I abruptly left the table and Brian wanted to follow. Joey on the other hand did not want Brian to follow.

I sprinted down the halls trying to decide where Gwen might be. The Bunker? No, too obvious. Her dorm? Doubtful, she had a roommate already that was always out though. Training room? Not likely at this time of the day. The roof! That had to be it. Our special spot.

Ok, I know what you are thinking. It's like our special spot to retreat to and just clear our heads. It was a good place to think. Plus, Headmaster Akhbar ok'd Gwen to create a greenhouse on the roof since she couldn't have one anywhere else.

I sprinted up the stair case and bumped into two kids, a son of Hades named Drake, and a son of Poseidon named Hady. They were arguing about whether or not some son of Thor could really lift his dad's hammer or not. *Psh!* That kid, Paris had a duplicate Mjölnir made. And he was real original with the name of it too. Mjölnir 2.0.

I pushed past them and had knocked a book out of Drake's hand. "Hey!" He angrily shouted. Hady had picked up the book back for him. I didn't have time for pleasantries with these two. *Oh well!*

I slammed through the door to the rooftop for no reason and skid on the pebbles lining the rooftop. I saw Gwen sitting in one of the adirondack chairs and gawked at my arrival. She had a glass of tea in her hand and I knew I was in trouble when the glass shattered against the floor. *Uh-oh!*

"Kyle! How dare you interrupt me introducing Nicole to

the campus!"

"Oh c'mon Gwen, you know I just wanted to say hi to our new member before I left." I faltered in my voice as Nicole stood up. Her hair was pitch black and her eyes were a piercing blue. Her gaze fixated on me, as if she was reading my soul.

She put her hand out to shake hands. "Nicole Ashby, daughter of Hades, and you are Kyle Pierce. Kyle's the douche right?"

Gwen smirked, "Correct!"

Douche? Ouch! I thought. Did Gwen really think of me like that now. Did I really just blow away a friendship all over some stupid book. Hecate was definitely going to hear from me after completing her errand.

I looked to the ground and kicked the pebbles back and forth. "You going to shake my hand douche?" Nicole said fiercely.

I shook her hand, "You and me are not going to be friends are we?"

"Not likely waterboy. You seem too wishy washy for my taste."

Gwen just sat and stared at the two of us.

"Just remember kid, disrespecting a friend has repercussions. Like a pebble being skipped in water, it causes ripples. Call me a ripple of your action to Gwen."

At this point our hand shake had turned into who could have a firmer grip, and a staring contest.

Gwen began to interlude, "Nicole, I can fight my own battles. You don't need to be mad at Kyle too, you just met."

"I can tell I already don't like this kid. I spent the past two years protecting the last nymph in Wisconsin. And let me tell you I protected Kalee with my whole heart!"

"Did you fail?" I asked curiously since Nicole's voice faltered.

"No, but I was reassigned. So I can no longer watch over my friend, and help keep her safe."

I let go of Nicole's hand as I saw tears well in her eyes. "Nicole, I can promise you now. If I am ever in Wisconsin for anything, I will go out of my way to look for Kalee and see if there is anything I can do to help her for you."

Nicole eyes were red, could a child of the Lord of the Dead truly cry? Could they feel sadness? I had always assumed they were emotionless. Guess you learn something every day.

Gwen looked at me wanting me to leave immediately. "Uhm, I am sorry for intruding, but I had wanted to say goodbye to you Gwen before I left for the quest. See you in about a week."

I tried to smirk but she sat there glaring at me. Nicole bowed her head and wished me luck. Ha, I would need luck now since I would be late with my meeting with Akhbar in fifteen minutes. And I still had no recollection of where his office was. I was a horrible student.

I sprinted down the stairwell hopping over the railing and sliding down others. I had made it to the 24th floor when I remembered there was an elevator on this half of the school.

I got to the elevator, and when the doors opened I saw the two kids from the stairwell whom I had ignored, Drake and Hady.

As I stepped into the elevator the two glared at me. The two held their small talk. They belonged to a little group we called the Brigand's. They were known for playing pranks on the students and sabotaging the school building. So being on an elevator with the two was not my favorite idea.

Hady spoke up, "Did you hear Daris was planning to plant a stink grenade in Chiron's ventilation system. Apparently it will stink up his whole office for weeks."

Drake smirked, "I heard it was to Akhbar. Either way it will beat what Keith did to Ethan last week with the water cups filling his room. How could he forget Ethan had power over water!"

I awkwardly stood there as the elevator Muzak played and

I stood between the two Brigander's. Which their name was funny since the name was a thief, not a prankster. But I'd rather their group pull pranks then become thieves. Jokes before crime.

The elevator finally dinged and I apologized for knocking Drake's book out of his hand and pushing the two. I bolted down the hallway in search of this elusive office. I looked at my watch, 12:04PM. Crap! I was late.

I creaked open the door and saw Joey to the left, and Brian to the right. The center chair was left open for myself. Akhbar sat with his chair swiveled facing the window.

"I was hoping you may have finally learned the concept of time, Kyle. But I can see my messenger failed at teaching you."

This guy was the definition of a dick. I was beginning to hope Daris had planted the stink bomb in the Headmaster's office.

"Pierce, why can you never be on time. Time efficiency is definitely your weak spot," Akhbar turned around in his chair with a sinister smile on his face. All he was missing was a fat cat in his lap and us calling him the Godfather.

Brian sat there with his bow at his feet, "Nor communicating with girls and showing emotions."

Akhbar's eyebrows ruffled themselves in confusion. "What?" He asked confused. "Never mind, back to the task at hand. It is important I understand what Loki instructed you to do."

"Is this like a requirement or something? I don't think I need to tell you what my mentor told me Headmaster." Something here was not right. Why was Akhbar curious with what Loki had told me?

"He gave us a-uh prophecy of sorts, Headmaster," Joey had a hesitation in his voice. He could sense that Akhbar's tone was growing darker.

"I requested to know what it is Joseph Schmitz! Tell me or I shall revoke your Bunker's status."

Joey sighed. Akhbar calling him by his full first name kinda shocked Brian and myself. I didn't even realize Joey's full name was Joseph, but it makes sense, like who is actually legally named Joey. Well, don't answer that cause I don't want to feel dumb. Maybe someone is named Joey on their birth certificate. I need to get back on track here!

Where were we, Joey sighing! Joey then began to speak. Then Brian jumped up, "Fine! I'll say it. The journey of three shall begin by sea. For one they must face their past. Another a sacrifice must be made. And the third, will stand alone in the end. For if more than three embark, they will not make it out together." Brian closed his eyes after saying it, as if he regretted opening his mouth.

Akhbar smiled, "So, between the three of you, one of you has kept a secret from the others, one will make a sacrifice, and the other alone. Seems like the three of you have your work cut out to get some simple book for Hecate."   He was enjoying our struggle.

He spun his chair back around, "I wish to speak with Joseph alone. I feel as though this new girl that has joined the Bunker has done so illegally. Has she not Mr. Schmitz?"

Brian had said, "No," simultaneously as Joey confessing that it indeed was.

"So our meeting will be justifiable then Joseph. I need to discuss other maters with you as well concerning upcoming events." He paused, and spun his chair back around. "The funny thing is, I have been vetoing and sanctioning quests for years now. You may have known this. Your Karkadann Incident was against the rules and I had to be forced to place a penalty upon your Bunker. Apparently you felt you could go behind my back years ago. And I knew Hecate wanted your team to tackle this quest. So she would've had it occur one way or another."

"So in other words, Hecate lost the book and you are trying to fix it before Athena finds out," Brian had nearly shot that option at Akhbar as an accusation.

"And I think you had a part in losing it. Perhaps?" I asked

He spun his chair back to the window, "My private affairs are none to your concern. Just accomplish your quest. And best of luck."

Brian and myself got up from our chairs and made our way to the door. As we opened the door and Brian had walked through Akhbar spoke once more, "Also Kyle. Be weary of Loki, he is not always a trustful god. You saw his castle, lonely and desolate. There is a reason he is alone now. Just don't blindly follow Loki into his tricks."

With that, we left the room with a bitter feeling in my gut. Brian and myself made our way to the Bunker, leaving Joey to deal with Akhbar.

CHAPTER 14

THROUGH THE REALMS WE GO

Brian stomped around the Bunker. He was mimicking the Headmaster. He the ranted, "I can't stand him! GARH!"

"Brian calm down," Gwen said walking through the doors. Nicole was next to her staring at Brian in confusion.

"I am perfectly calm Gwendolyn Mahoney!" Brian mocked her. "I'm sorry my brother is getting bitched at by the Headmaster for her joining the 4921 without doing the process. And did you know we are still on probation technically?"

Gwen walked up to Brian and slapped him across the face. He gawked for a moment, "What the f-"

"Language!" she said aggressively. "No cursing in front of Jim and Tim. Bunker rule. And never call me by my full name Schmitz. Or else I will-"

"So," I quickly interjected before Gwen could further her threat. "Good to you see you again Ashby."

"No comment, aside from you two making great first

impressions." Nicole's voice was heavy with annoyance. "You two are just peachy additions to the Bunker. I think Gwen and I will enjoy babysitting the twins, and not corrupting them like you two do."

"Wow Nicole, is Hades as ignorant as you are? I haven't met him yet but I feel like he has a nicer personality then you. Spend too much time in the Underworld?"

"To hell with you!" she said as she marched away. Gwen followed suit.

"Yeah, walk away! We will just be in here with the TV." Brian's shouting was stupid. The girls could cut the power at any moment if either of them wanted to.

"Brian," I said softly so the girls could not hear.

"Yeah?" He said quite loudly.

"The girls definitely do not like us anymore."

Brian made a face, followed by two or three more. "Nope, you're right. Fair enough. And in our defense we don't like them either."

I shook my head rubbing my eyes. Joey was taking a while. And with how long it was taking it may be later in the day then we had hoped to leave for the quest. It was getting close to dusk.

***

After sitting idle for more than three hours and missing dinner in fear Joey would arrive, he had finally showed up in the Bunker. His eyes were red. He had definitely been crying. But what about?

"You two ready to go?" Joey asked.

"We've been ready for the past few hours. What did you talk to Akhbar about?" Brian quizzically asked.

"Not important right now. All that matters is that we get to the portal and go meet Hermes, or he meets us. Whatever the process is truly. I've had both occur."

I looked around amused, "So Nicole. She's just a ray of sunshine isn't she?"

"Look she came to us. I saw her résumé and I had to accept. Her work out protecting that Nymph was amazing. She has the spirit of a true Bunker 4921 member." Joey seemed excited about her future in the Bunker. He knew something, that the rest of us were unaware of.

"Debatable," I murmured under my breath. Nicole was still not going to be a friend of mine. "Anyways let's go."

The three of us grabbed our bags and boarded the elevator. The elevator ride was filled with silence. None of us wanted to talk.

As the doors opened Phil, and two other Roman demigods stood to either side of his. One had an eyepatch covering one of his eyes. Phil chuckled, "Good to see the Bunker is still later than us. Joey, you're meeting with the Headmaster delayed us from leaving sooner. Yet, how is it we are still leaving before you."

"Now listen here blondie, I'm not playing down to your level. I am older therefore I will be mature about this situation and ignore you."

Phil and his colleagues laughed briefly, "Ha, then where are your friends to send you off? Couldn't be bothered? Or did they fear being catapulted as well?"

Catapulted? What was Stryker talking about?

"None of your business, and it is time we let this feud go Phil!"

"Not happening anytime soon Schmitz. I was told Hermes is waiting for you all since he has the Realms ready to go. That way you children of the sun don't get to dizzy in there."

Brian stuck his tongue out as we walked out of the door. I wish we didn't have to see them as our last demigod acquaintances of this place. It was going to make it hard to wanna come back.

As we reached the edge of the Realm the door opened before us and Hermes walked out, "Hello demigods! Joey, Brian, and Kyle I presume? I am Hermes, Greek god of, well lots of stuff. A messenger of the gods, but also a god of travelers. And it was my shift in the Portal Realm this week.

Well, it is usually my shift now. Heimdall gets to just sit at the Sky Cliffs and watch over Asgard and their Bifrost. Eh oh well. Now where do you need to go?"

I stepped forward, "Well Lord Hermes, we were thinking Washington D.C., United States of America."

Hermes teetered his head, "I can do Cape Henlopen State Park, Delaware. It's near Rehoboth Beach, but it is a State Park so it is a less crowded beach and the sand is so nice. I can place you all there with a car in the parking lot too."

"Wait Hermes, isn't there one closer then Delaware," Joey asked concerned.

"Yes, but what fun is a quest without a little journey? Oh be aware of the feeling of vertigo. People have been complaining of it recently. I am looking into it. Or well not me but Vulcan is, and it's-"

Hermes was cut off from the portal sucking us through it.

***

I know I love the beach and all. It is my happy place after all, but falling into it from a portal that already made you dizzy was not fun. Especially since I had to rescue an unconscious Joey before he drowned.

As I swam Joey and myself to shore I realized how cold the water actually was. It was only spring. I shivered and then imagined how cold they must have been. We looked around and noticed the beach was deserted.

106

I splashed some water on Joey's face and he screamed as he came through.

"Where, where are we?" he stammered.

"We are at a beach, just like Loki said. The journey shall begin by sea. Anyone else think Loki should not have been allowed to decide the prophecy wording or let Hermes man the Portal Realm. Two pranksters," Brian had a bit of annoyance in his voice. I had thought Brian liked pranks.

Joey looked cold and distant, "Let's go find a place in the woods to go build a fire and get warm. Also we can sleep there and fine a way to D.C. in the morning."

CHAPTER 15

THE TALE OF THE POWERHOUSE

Joey had decided it was best we make camp for the night instead of trekking onwards. He had an irritable look in his eye's ever since we left Demigod Central.

I knew he had had a talk with Headmaster Akhbar, but other than that I didn't know what may have been bothering him. Maybe it was the contents of their talk? Or was it seeing Phil before leaving?

Brian snapped his bow in half and began to fiddle with his blades. Poking each one into the small embers Joey was trying to make into a fire.

Brian finally decided to break the silence after some time of awkward silence, "So since it's just us broski's, what do you all wanna talk about?" He leaned back against a tree and crossed his arms. The small licks of fire curling up illuminated his face in a menacing way.

Joey gave him a side glance, "What in the name of Tartarus is a broski?"

Brian scratched his chin momentarily, as if he himself was

pondering the thought. Then he broke the cricket chirps with his response, "Well it's like girls, how they got their best friends forever. It's like the dude version. We're bros that would do anything for the other. And why do you always need to bring everything to Tartarus? Can't we go to the name of Zeus, Hades, Neptune, Sif, or you know Wi?"

Joey gave his brother one of the stupidest annoyed looks I had ever seen. "That is idiotic. Why not just say bros?"

"Because broski sounds better to me. Maybe it's a personal preference." Brian smirked as he had managed to defeat his brother. I couldn't help but chuckle. "So Kyle, tough choice leaving Gwen behind. Seemed to bother you last night. Have a nightmare?"

Joey turned his attention to me as well. "What? No, that wasn't about her! Look, I didn't have much of a choice. We needed someone to stay back and lead the Bunker for us." Silently Joey shook his head. "You know what I find interesting though. Why did Akhbar give the go ahead for two searching quests, for the first time in several years, on the same day. It's been years, really since our Karkadann Incident."

Brian began to laugh, "Yeah especially to Phil and his Legionnaires. Psh, those self righteous pricks."

The look on Joey's face as Brian had mention Phil sent a jolt up and down my spine. As though I had just gotten electrocuted again. Joey and Phil didn't get along. Anyone could see that. I had my reasons for not liking the kid, but it was time I learned why Joey didn't.

"Joey, what do you have against Phil Stryker exactly?" I asked.

He lowered his head. "Look, I don't have to like everyone at our school, do I? You don't like him either."

Brian scoffed, "Yeah, but what about that one kid who toured the Bunker. Our little test subject. Back when we had just started and got Gwen. We were trying to get that Roman."

The sigh that came out of Joey's mouth, may have been one of the deepest regrets I had ever heard. As if air in his lungs was being ripped out of him slowly, failing to be replenished. Joey had always struck me as protective and reserved. I had assumed this was because of him caring so deeply for Brian without his parents help. No, I knew there was something deeper that lurked inside of him, guilt.

"Fine," Joey's head lowered and a menacing glow danced across his face from the fire. "Seven years ago, when I was tasked with forming Bunker 4921, I needed recruits. We couldn't just have a few demigods housing that large bunker."

His breath had steadied and slowed as if processing the events in his head. "The kid was barely younger than me at the time. So he couldn't have been more than 12. The kid was a tank. I had never seen a fighter as skilled as this kid was."

I rested my head on my arm, beginning to hunch over to continue listening to the story. "What happen?"

Joey licked his lips and began to continue, "This kid, Isaac, he was a son of Mars. Chiron had approached me and asked me to show him around. He felt as though he would fit well with us. Yet Phil Stryker, gosh he's what a year older than you two. So he'd be 10, and this kid was already in charge of the centuries old Legionaries. He was the best of the best for the Romans, and he expected the best Romans to be with him as well."

I shifted uneasily, "Well, what happened then?"

"Phil knew my past, and what I had done. The wrong deals I had made. He didn't agree with me and thought I was corrupted. Me and him became rivals quickly after him learning my history."

His history? What was Joey talking about? He had always told me when he was little him and Brian would go around the United States looking for sanctuary. Joey always protecting Brian. Joey was a protective older brother. I began to wonder what he had meant by his wrong deals.

"Phil got frustrated I got to give Isaac the tour. I was busy trying to persuade Isaac he needed to join the Bunker over the Legionnaires. I had done a bit more than persuading as well. I had come across a group of Hermes, Mercury, and Loki kids all pulling pranks, you know their usual stunts. They were doing it in the school hall, which was against the rules. So, I had them help me out, and I wouldn't rat on them. I had decided it was best to humiliate Phil once it was his turn to talk to Isaac. I thought that would show Isaac the Legionnaires were nothing but a laughing stock."

I tried to imagine Joey doing any of this but it slipped my mind. He seemed too tranquil and protective to have done this.

"We set up the prank to embarrass Phil enough that he would become enraged and show the side of him that turns people away. We set up a trip wire followed by pie catapults."

The pie catapults! I had seen those things in the back room of the Bunker when I had done some exploring. I wasn't necessarily supposed to be there, but yeah, I sorta did anyways. I figured I'd one day be in charge so I might as well know all the little tricks and what not.

"We had waited for him to enter the Grand Hall Entrance. He was wearing his purple cloak as well. He was dressed to impress and show his rank. The gloating little dweeb."

Joey uncapped a bottle of water and began to gulp some down. "Sorry, this fire's smoke is dehydrating me some. Where was I, oh yeah. So he's entering the Grand Hall and me and the prankster kids had set up this elaborate embarrassing trap."

Brian began to chuckle. "Gods the end of this story is the best. But not the way you tell it."

"The trap would've been perfect."

"Would have been?" I asked in confusion. "What went wrong?"

Brian chuckled and Joey shot him a stern look. "What went wrong? It's stupid what went wrong, and I don't know how I didn't think it could've happened. Isaac walked in first. The trap was set up that when Phil walked in the trip wire would spring into action. It would release the pie catapults all aimed on him. Except it wasn't pie we had primed it with. We used several cornucopia's."

"You mean those wicker basket things they use at Thanksgiving?" I quizzically asked.

"Well, yeah, except the cornucopia's didn't necessarily produce anything. They were all duds. And the prankster kids all screwed up in thinking that through. Instead they had all been thrown at Isaac injuring the poor kid. One of the cornucopias had hit him dead in the eye. So, now he walks around with an eyepatch to cover his blood-filled eyeball. Isaac was outraged and nearly destroyed the Grand Hall in his rampage. It was all my fault, and now he is half-blind."

The fire crackled and we all sat in silence. Well, for someone who had lived at the school for so long I had not heard of much of these events. Chiron left me sheltered, and I was beginning to wonder why. Something he had once told me was to be careful asking the wrong questions around the wrong people. I was wondering who these, "Wrong people" were now.

Joey looked around and then spoke softly, "Make sure we are quiet. We will continue moving out in the morning. For now we will just make camp here. Get some sleep guys. I'll wake everyone up in the morning."

CHAPTER 16

ALL THAT IS GOLD DOES NOT ALWAYS GLITTER

Typical me. I said I would not focus my dreams, but I was curious. I racked my brain for anything I had ever heard of Chrysaor. If he was with Vivian and they had the book. It was best I read up on my opponent.

My mind flashed through time, similar to the vertigo I felt when going through the Portal Realm.

I stood on a cliffside. The waves lapsed against the cliff, splashing water over the edge of the eroding cliff. As I looked around I noted a wrecked temple. Snakes were heard hissing around the area. I walked over the edge and saw a pool of blood being washed into the ocean.

Now in old time mythology, whenever blood went into the water, something bad usually came about it. And I'm just gonna say it now, I blame my dad.

As I sat down against the edge and had my feet dangle. I wonder, what would come from this blood. Just then, the ocean began to fizz. Not good. I searched my mind for the creatures that had come from the ocean. I felt like an old computer that Chiron kept trying to pass off as new, and searching on it, and having a website break the computer because it was so old and bad at processing. This was my mind right. I was that processor.

Just then a winged horse flew out of the fizz and whinnied. Pegasus! Which meant, I was at the birth of... Chrysaor. A dark hand grabbed the cliff head next to me clasping onto a headless body. Medusa's body.

He laid the body down and a tear fell from his eye. "Mother?" His voice was soft, weak, and full of pain.

Pegasus hovered above him whinnying uselessly, at least to my ear. Chrysaor turned to Pegasus with a face full of tears, "How can you be so remorseless you beast! Mother is dead and you only care of your new found freedom. Think about her. Think about the monster that did this to her!"

Pegasus whinnied once more. Chrysaor's eyebrow twitched. He actually seemed to be understanding what his horse of a brother was saying. "You suggest we hunt the monster? I like your style brother. Perhaps we consider this method and bring mother her head back for a proper burial."

He pondered the idea and looked back at Pegasus, "I like this plan, but I must train first. Then we can get revenge on this monster. I want you to go and befriend this killer of mother and I will whistle when I am trained well enough."

Pegasus whinnied and flew upward into the clouds and vanished.

Time fast forward and I felt the vertigo coming. Bleh!

I sat in a field littered with old broken weapons. A few skeletons of numerous species littered the area. A young half-horse half-man sat watching two men in combat. I looked intently at the centaur and realized I was gazing out at a young Chiron. He was teaching Chrysaor who was now taller and wore a golden chest plate and leg pads. His sparing partner looked familiar as well. My mind was still getting back to this time. Looking at the face the partner was Heracles.

Chrysaor was training with Chiron and Heracles!

The fight ended with Chrysaor disarming Heracles and retrieving his sword he went to hand it back to his partner. "Haha no my friend, you have fairly won that blade. Keep her, she will do good among you and your righteous battle to avenge your mother."

Chrysaor tilted the blade, "A mighty sword, but this color does not suit me, perhaps gold?"

Chiron chuckled, "You know where Midas lives Chrysaor. Just call upon your brother and have him fly you to Midas' desolate kingdom."

"Wise words Chiron. Need any other errands while I am out?"

"No I will be good, thank you though."

Chrysaor walked out to a hill and whistled three times. Pegasus bolted down from the clouds and whinnied repeatedly.

Chrysaor's expression was full of anger. "We must make haste then my brother. Midas can wait for now. Off to find this monster. Go!"

He mounted Pegasus and bolted into the clouds. Somehow I was tied to Chrysaor and levitated throughout the clouds alongside my half-brother's. Pegasus was only in the air briefly before beginning his descent. Within moments we landed on a rocky terrain.

Upon arriving to a cliff edge stood a young boy and an elderly man. The boy was yelling at his grandfather. "You have wronged us and our kingdom for too long grandfather. You knew what the Oracle foretold of Perseus!"

Perseus gazed past his grandson and upon Pegasus. He called out, "My friend Pegasus, rescue me. I need your help. We must get to safety."

From behind Pegasus, Chrysaor emerged with his golden armor plated on his body. His dark skin made the armor radiate even brighter. "My name is Chrysaor. You killed my mother, and secretly my brother and I have plotted your death ever since that very moment you killed her many years ago."

Perseus chuckled, "Oh dear, you must be mistaken. Your brother is not a flying horse my friend, and I do not kill people."

Pegasus whinnied furiously. Chrysaor looked at his brother. Chrysaor's face twitched, "You mean my mother was a monster? No...no! She was a..."

"A monster. She terrorized people for years. I sliced her head off because she was a gorgon. Look for any story of Medusa boy. You will learn the truth."

"Where is her head? Where is it?" Chrysaor had tears rolling down his face down. His muscles rippled as they tensed. He was growing angry.

"I burned it years ago so it could never hurt any mortal again. Nothing remains of her head!"

As Perseus was saying that his grandson had impaled him with an old blade. "The blade you used to slay Medusa will be what ends you as well. You may have stopped Medusa and the Kraken, but you are still a horrible person.

The dream became augmented. The land seemed to go on forever. The moment froze. Chrysaor walked over to the dying Perseus and clutched him in his hands. The grandson and Pegasus were no where to be seen. I suddenly realized this was Chrysaor's memory and he was so focused everything else ceased to exist.

"I was supposed to kill you and avenge my mother. My

life goal, and I have failed."

Perseus coughed holding onto to his last breath, "You realize anything you do, you cannot break the Oracle's prophecy, nor Fate. Do not tempt to alter either of those Chrysaor. We are all meant for something, and I was destined to die by my own kin. You, you were always meant to be a monster. I was foretold an eternal life in the stars upon death, and you I will always look down at you upon nights and haunt you. I will remind you, you are no hero, you are born of a monster. You are the Golden Warrior. I will never let you find sanctuary. And when your time comes your head will be severed as well."

"I should crush you in my hands. And truly crush the life out of you." Tears were streaming down his face as he tried to maintain a threatening appearance.

"Do it, and prove the villain you truly are."

As Perseus had said that, his life faded. Chrysaor pushed the body away from him. The dream began to fall apart like a broken mirror. Each shard depicting Chrysaor throughout the years. Cutting off Midas' hand. Fighting against other gladiators in the Roman Colosseum. Standing next to Egyptian Pharaohs. Leading Nordic Berserkers. And fighting in the Revolutionary War against the British.

I sat upright in my sleep as the last shard shattered leaving me in darkness. "Morning sunshine," Joey said. "Care if we start driving?"

I realized we had a long drive ahead of us trying to leave the beach on a Sunday. Sitting in traffic we heard people with their windows down talking about some Bridge spanning a bay, the Bay Bridge? They said it was awful on weekends like this. *Great*, a long car ride ahead of us. And more importantly the thought of Chrysaor lingering in my mind. Even looking out the window in the slow speed of our car would not be able to take the thought of what I had seen out of my mind.

CHAPTER 17

THE DINER THAT
WENT BOOM

After driving around aimlessly for about three hours we finally decided to stop and get some food. Which I don't know about the others, but I was starving.

We decided to pull off of Route 50 and go to a town called Crofton, Maryland. And lucky for us this was not too far out of our way, but personally I wish we had stopped off at the Greek restaurant we had past back by Annapolis, instead of looking for some diner. But for some reason Brian was set on finding this diner in particular.

Joey was not the best driver around, and I feel as though he knew it. He was constantly five miles under the speed limit. And drivers around this area were full of road rage. They were easily going 65 to 75 in the 50 mph zone. I feared for my life on several occasions with him as the driver.

The car finally came to a stop in the diner's parking lot. "We are here," he had said with a bit of a sigh in his voice. He looked back at us, "Alright so who's hungry?"

As we walked into the diner everything seemed normal.

An average amount of middle aged people drinking bland coffee and reading the newspaper. A few out of style dressed waitresses walked around refilling the coffee for their patrons. Some even knew each other by name.

Out of everything in this diner there was only one thing that seemed out of place. And Brian sat us at the counter directly across from him. Brian just sat there with a smug smile on his face. The man's name tag on his apron read Mr. Kapre. The man looked at Brian with a strike of annoyance and a toothpick resting in his mouth, "May I help you kid."

Brian sat there like a giddy school girl. What had gotten into him?

As I looked back towards Mr. Kapre, I noticed he was now smoking a pipe. He was about 7-feet tall and had a dark complexion. His skin reminded me of tree bark at times.

Brian finally broke his trance by saying, "Ah yes, I'd like some fried rice with chicken dumplings and three egg rolls please."

Mr. Kapre just bowed his head slightly and left without taking anyone else's order. Yup, definitely on my strange list now. And talk about your 5 star service.

He came back almost instantaneously with his food. This was getting stranger by the second. Mr. Kapre began to blow smoke rings in front of us. While Brian chowed down on his food, I caught Joey staring outside at something. Whatever it was, Joey seemed to be in a trance.

I looked to Joey and finally spoke up, "Hey Joey, what you looking at bud?"

I gave him a nudge and he finally said, "Hunh? Uh, not sure, but I realized I have to go somewhere."

The man behind the counter looked at me with distaste, "You're inquiring about your friend's oddness, hunh boy."

I looked back towards the man and shook my head. Brian was still in his food trance eating everything in sight, and well Joey was staring off into no man's land it seemed. I was slowly realizing that this little diner had entrancing characteristics. Brian's was food. Joey's was staring into the distance. The elderly, it was their coffee and newspapers. Mr. Kapre knew this too.

I turned around and he was gone.

I slowly got off of my stool and motioned towards my backpack to unsheathe Shadow. With my sword in hand I felt a little bit more safe, but still on edge. I walked behind the counter and began to walk towards the back room. I could see a faint little white light coming from behind the door.

Now here was the question, would I continue going all cautious, or be rash and kick in the door. Now if you chose choice number 2 you'd be correct. I'm very rash when it comes down to it. I think on impulse not precautions. Which is going against every training advice Gwen has given me.

I kicked in the door and saw the 7 foot giant Mr. Kapre huddled behind a desk staring at a white gleaming stone. He slowly stood up from behind the desk and said, "So you are going to take it from me too? Everyone who doesn't fall into my trance tries."

"Uhm, what?" I asked in confusion.

"Like those before you, you have come here to steal what is mine. However I will not let this happen boy. I will find your weakness. The archer's, his was easy it was food. His brother, I lucked out with. His mind showed me what he feared easily. Not even my prying. It was just there for the picking."

"What did you show him? What is his fear?" I asked a bit more on edge. My sword tip was now pointed at him. I had a feeling Mr. Kapre might be a bit more dangerous than I had expected.

"To Hades if I know boy, I only made it seem like a reality to him. I didn't actually pry. I used it to lure him like I lure all." He began to caress the rock in his hand. If I wanted him to talk I may need to take the little stone from him.

"What are you then, Mr. Kapre?" I began to creep closer while side stepping the room. He would notice soon enough what I was up to. Hopefully it gave me time to think of something to do though.

He chuckled a bit amused, "You must be from Demigod Central. They still haven't expanded their education system have they? Still stuck on the Greeks, Romans, and Norse I take it." I was almost in position, but I'd rather know what I was up against before I'd strike.

"You see they don't teach you about the smaller sects of mythology boy. Your knowledge is bland when it comes to the universe of it all. These Realms, yeah they divide it to hide some of them well. Why do you think Hermes guards the gate?"

"You are getting off topic Mr. Kapre. Who and what are you?"

"I have already told you, have I not? My name is Mr. Kapre. I am a Kapre."

My mind raced like a thousand horses racing along the race track, each one trying to out run the other. My forward advancement began to turn into a bit of a retreat.

Mr. Kapre just chuckled. "You don't know what a Kapre is do you boy? Well, I'll enlighten you. We are a mythological creature that comes from the Philippines. We are tree demons. We breath fire, hence the constant pipe. And this stone grants those who can take it away a wish. And as a downside my skin is tree bark. I am a tree spirit of sorts."

Now Nicole had mentioned a Nymph named Kalee. Nicole seemed to like Kalee, implying she was nice and all. Mr. Kapre would not fall into the nice category of plant spirits.

"Well, I don't want your little wish granting pebble or anything. I just want to grab my friends and leave. We have an important mission to attend to and we've been held up here long enough."

"Funny, cause you all are not getting the chance to leave." Mr. Kapre began to close in on me now. He swung his fist now clenching his pebble tightly. His fist caught me in the side sending me flying towards the bookcase along the wall. Leave it to me to get backhanded by a giant tree demon.

His hand was rough like tree bark as well. Kapre's were not something I wanted to mess around with.

I quickly scuttled around the floor to grab Shadow. I stuck it in his side and an agonizing yell shot out from within him. I'm pretty positive half of the diner heard it. And in fact they did. You could hear panic and commotion fill the diner. The people had snapped out of their hypnotic state and were fleeing the building.

Good, I thought to myself. If they had left the building that meant me and Mr. Kapre could have a good old showdown now.

I gripped Shadow firmly in my hand and waited for him to make the next move. I heard Brian and Joey running to find me. I saw Brian sprint past the door, trip, and fall on his face. He picked himself up and ran into the room wielding his short swords. Smart this was going to be a close combat fight, and my longsword wouldn't be good for that much longer.

"Three demigods who want to steal my rock. Funny cause it only grants one wish, and to whomever gets it first."

Joey stared at the Kapre intensely. "Kyle, what were you thinking trying to fight a Kapre on your own."

I looked at him with a bit of annoyance. My sword lowered a bit, "Joey, you were too busy staring at your big fear. You were in a daze. Just like Brian was with his food."

Brian burped as if on cue, "Yea, I'm regretting eating so much. But hey, I do love my Chinese food. Speaking of which, Mr. Kapre, could I get your recipe for the egg rolls?"

"BRIAN!" Joey and myself snapped instantly.

"What, I just wanted his recipe. Those were really good. I really wanna know," Brian put his short swords back together, forming his bow and slung it over his shoulders. "Now, Mr. Kapre, I apologize for my brother and friend's behavior. It was uncalled for. We don't want to take your stone. In matter of fact I'll hold onto it for you. So you can beat them into a pulp."

"BRIAN!" Joey snapped louder and a bit angrier this time.

The Kapre just smiled. Brian's plan was working. The Kapre handed Brian his stone. "Hold onto this for me while I beat your friends into a bloody stew."

"Gladly," Brian said with a mischievous smirk. Brian slid the stone into his pocket. "And one last thing Mr. Kapre," Brian began to add. "This stone is good after your death too, right? Works with resurrections as well?"

He turned and faced Brian, "Why yes they are, and, wait. You son of a -"

Mr. Kapre's curses were cut short by Joey's knife sticking him in the leg. He crumpled in pain. He swung his branch of an arm striking Joey in the side. Mr. Kapre stood up and looked down at me and let out a breath of fire. Brian was helping Joey to his feet as we all began to make a run for it.

Brian took Joey towards the front exit. I headed for the rooftop hatch. And I know what you are probably thinking, run for the roof? WHY? Well, yeah. I needed to get him away from my friends. Protecting what I cared about.

I climbed the ladder at a quickened pace. Carefully grabbing every other rung as holding Shadow presented a difficulty in climbing. Maybe I needed to consider getting a new blade. Upon reaching the top I sprinted towards the edge.

Just then fire bellowed up behind me. I turned around to see the Kapre itself. His apron was now gone. It revealed his torn torso of old tree bark. He had on a loin cloth and his pipe was in his hands. "You see kiddo, there ain't too many places to hide in trees around here."

"So you adapted and made this diner?"

"Precisely. Now you are catching on. Too bad you ruined everything!"

"Eh, I'm a demigod, you're a monster harming others. I can't let that happen. Plus you tried keeping my friends. That is the real no no."

He smirked at me, "Either way you die here kid. If I go down you go down. You jump, you die. It ends here for you."

I wished Brian were here. He had the stone that could make all of this stop. But Brian was busy escorting his brother out of the diner to safety. I came to the realization that if I was going to stand a chance in a fight, I couldn't use Shadow.

I unzipped my backpack and sheathed my sword. The tree man continued to smile, "Giving up the fight so easily I see?"

"Not exactly," I was eyeing the boiler system on the roof. I might be able to get him to bring down his building. "See I had this idea. What if you tried to kill me up here instead? But you can only use your fire breath three times."

"An interesting proposal kid."

"Kyle," I said frantically trying to delay him. "You might as well know my name so when I die here you can say, 'I am the mighty Kapre, slayer of Kyle.' Bet you that sounds much better than killer of some demigod kid."

I caught him in my ploy. I could see him thinking. Now I just needed to make sure two of those breaths hit the boiler system. "I accept this offer Kyle. This shall be fun. A little close quarter combat for the half-blood, and I get to use my fire. Haven't done that in a while."

"Good me either." I tossed my backpack off of the roof towards the car. Hopefully Brian or Joey would see it and grab it for me.

I inched my way left towards the boiler system. This would be a cakewalk I began to think. Then it hit me that if this plan worked, yeah I'd bring down the building, but also myself. I had only half thought this plan through, and I'd need to change up some of my ideas.

Too late.

Just then the first breath of flame was released. I had narrowly escaped it as it hit the boiler system. The system began to hiss. I needed to move quickly. Likewise I had also failed to think that even one breath could be a ticking time bomb against this building. Wait! That's what I needed. If I stalled the Kapre I could manage to get the building to blow and jump to safety. Or mostly safety.

I crept towards him so we were at about the center of the

roof. "Bring it on Mr. Kapre!"

He opened his mouth releasing the next wave of flames behind me. I ducked trying to avoid it but he was counting on me doing so. This breath was meant to encase me in a half-circle of flames.

He swung the first punch and I side stepped it. I barreled my body into his gut sending him backwards.

He stood up off of the boiler system as I backed up slowly. "Haha you fool. You damned fool. You thought you could simply beat me like that?"

"No, I could never beat a Tree Genie." I saw how close the boiler system was to blowing so I snapped and bolted away from him. His last breath of fire chased after me. But I heard the explosion as I jumped from the building.

All I saw was a bright white light on my descent. The fire had engulfed the building like I had planned and everything began to tumble to the earth with me. I just prayed I wouldn't get crush by the debris.

I landed against the doorstep as the roof collapsed on the diner. No one was left in there except the now deceased Mr. Kapre. Everyone was accounted for.

I was kind of upset for Brian. He didn't get to use his one wish. I wonder if it would travel from a monsters life to life. If the next Mr. Kapre would still honor the fact that Brian had his stone, or if it was a new stone too. The Kapre had never answered him.

I laid back in the rubble, wounded and sore, taking in the fact of what I had just done. A bit exhausted. But I had done it.

CHAPTER 18

WE SPY ON A CORPORATION

The funny thing is, I felt nothing. The wound on my shoulder, the cut on my hip. None of that mattered. I had proven myself a hero. Well, kinda. If blowing up a diner that stops some evil tree genie. Then yeah, I am a hero. But, I had taken down a Kapre's base where it lured people to an eternal routine of diner coffee and soup. Yet the one person I wanted to celebrate the most with wasn't here. Sure I had Brian and Joey. But that wasn't the same. I wanted to look Gwen in the eyes and hug her. I had to admit it to myself after that, I definitely had a massive crush on Gwen.

Ok, I know what you are thinking, *you're the idiot who pushed her away.* Well, yeah, but I was stupid!

Brian and Joey walked through the rubble pulling me up to my feet. Smoke still whisked in the air as ash still fell to the earth.

Brian wiped the soot from his face. "Next time, can you not let me get Chinese food from a diner. Like that, or just not from a psychotic fire breathing whatever that thing was."

Joey just laughed, "Funny cause that's an easier one runt."

We continued walking as Brian stopped in confusion, "Wait! An easier one? That was an easy one? What is a hard one then? Please tell me it isn't something that doesn't require an explosion to be killed."

We got back in the car and drove towards D.C. The drive was not too long and filled mostly with silence. Joey had grown tense since whatever Mr. Kapre had shown him back there.

In the distance we had passed through the beltway. As I looked out of my window I could see the little skyline that was Washington D.C. I had seen it in pictures and in textbooks. The Washington Monument, an obelisk that stood towards the center of the city. "It's impressive," I said in awe.

"It's where we need to find a book," Brian said sarcastically.

Joey kept driving through the city not showing any signs of slowing down or driving with any true purpose. "Not yet," he stammered. "I need to meet with an associate of mine first."

Brian looked at him tense momentarily, and then eased his gaze back to his window. Nothing was said, but I got the message. Brian knew what Joey was doing, and whatever it was he did not like it.

He pulled around to the outskirts of the city, a less populated area at least. I looked around and saw nothing but a skyscraper and it's fenced in parking lot with the security guard station serving as the only entrance or exit. Joey rolled our vehicle up to the checkpoint and the guard looked at us sternly. "Identification or turn around kids."

Brian rolled his eyes, "Always calling us kids. I am almost 17, sir, I think it is time I get referred to as a teenager or a young adult."

The guard got out of his station and began walking over to Brian's side of the car. "Get out of the vehicle now. All of you!" The guard shouted in a not so friendly manner.

Joey quickly got out of the car and walked up to the guard and whispered something in his ear. Brian was secretly clutching his knife waiting for the cue to strike. The guard scoffed and walked back to his station and rose the barrier allowing us to enter.

Joey drove the car forward and parked in an open spot with cars on either side. "Look, I need you two to stay put for a moment. I have someone I need to talk with real quick. I'll be right back."

I sat forward like a bolt of lightning and put my hand on Joey's shoulder, "Does this have anything to do with the diner. It looked as though Mr. Kapre had begun to show you something. You were caught in a daze looking out the window."

Joey ripped my arm off of his shoulder. "If it did, I don't want you all getting involved. I just need to talk with someone really quick. Stay put." And with that he slammed the car door and bolted towards the buildings door.

As Joey walked into the building the doors shut behind him and made a locking noise. Not an ideal building that I would want to go into.

Continuing to look around the area, I began to not like the looks of it all the more. He was already nervous and why did he lead us directly to the building he was going to just end up leaving us in the car? There was something more to Joey's story that he was not sharing with us.

Brian stared in agony watching his brother walk away from him. "I'm following him," Brian said as he fiddled with his bow slung across his shoulder. It had somehow managed to get tangled up in his seat belt with him.

I had never actually seen Brian worried like this. Usually he was care free and willing to do what his brother said. But recently Joey had been more secretive and had been hiding stuff from us, and even Brian.

Brian began to feel betrayed by his brother. I could see it in his face. His eyes began to twitch and his face grew emotionless. He was now dead-set determined to figure out what his brother was up to.

I knew that trying to tell him no wouldn't work, or be so simple. "Let's go see what is inside then Brian."

***

Going in the front door would obviously get us detected immediately so we had searched for another entrance into this fort of a building. We had found one service exit but it was locked with keycard access only.

The two of us were in the back of the building with no way in other than a locked door. We looked around a bit more until Brian saw an air vent. "Hold still and watch out for any guards to come by, cause I'm gonna go unlock the hatch."

I was shouting in a hushed tone, which if you think about it is like a whisper shout, "No we are not crawling through an air shaft to find Joey! Brian! Brian, don't!"

Too late on my part, he had already parkoured up to the air vent and began using an arrow head to unscrew the cap from the building.

After a minute he threw the vent cover to the ground. "Alright c'mon. We don't have that much time."

Crawling through an air shaft was definitely a low point of this day. It had already been so exciting and action filled, that this...it just seemed sub par.

We came across an air vent that showed us the lobby. Three muscular men in black uniforms with full blown utility belts, equipped with tasers, handcuffs, pistols, extra magazines, and assault riffles slung across their backs. In between them stood a doctor with a dark lab coat as well.

Why did what appeared to be bad guys always wear dark clothing? I would love to see a bad guy wear neon one time. Or even a pastel color. Like is this too much to ask for?

I noticed each of them had a patch stitched to their left arms. It had a lion head, with wings and a scorpion tail encompassing what appeared to be a globe of latitude and longitude lines.

"Can you believe these guys!" Brian was pretty adamant about his opinion about these guys. "These guys are part of a PMC. And their soldiers are equipped with ARX-160's. Dicks!"

"Brian, *shhhh!* They are talking let's try to hear what they have got to say."

The scientist had a Croatian accent to him. And yes don't mock me because I can pinpoint an accent. I had a class on it, and I actually paid attention to it. "-you do not understand. We need to speak to your acting officer on this location. Our latest experiments, as worn by these three officers, will show you that they can identify this, hybrid breed of humans you wish to call Half-Blood's. It is still in a prototype phase, but so far with the subjects blood you have provided, we have acquired nine other test subjects. And we are working on developing the devices further, in order to learn and manipulate the powers this hybrid breed has and we can replicate it and use it against them." The doctor looked urgent in his use of hand gestures. Either it was urgent, or he was a great puppeteer.

The man at the desk nodded his head, "Look Dr., erh, what was your name again?"

"Doctor Marik!" The doctor's temper was beginning to flare.

"My boss, is in a meeting with an old associate right now, but I am sure he will be more than willing to meet you if you schedule an appointment. Mr. M is a very busy man as you must imagine."

"Manticore Global's employees wait for no one! Let Morpheus know I will be paying him a visit soon!" The guards walked in a triangle formation as Dr. Marik stormed out

Brian looked at me and shrugged his shoulders. That was definitely was something we needed to discuss later on.

It took us a while but we had finally found an elevator shaft and made our way to the top floor. Gosh, this building had too many floors. As we crawled through the air shaft, the path seemed to go on forever until we had finally got an eye on Joey. Or at least Brian did. He froze and just watched his brother converse. All I heard was the echoes that made it into the air vent.

"Look, I paid my dues and I served my time. I will contact you when I finish my task. But I am done working for you all."

"Working? For us? Try, us saving your life kid. We took you in and helped you survive! Now you will repay your debt in full and we will release you when we see fit!"

"Yes, yes sir."

The conversation concluded and Joey had walked out of the office. Uh-oh! That was our cue to get back to the car before he did. Which we definitely had more obstacles then needed.

We had almost made it back to the elevator shaft, and I began to have the urge to sneeze. Brian was already too far ahead of me to notice. He was on his decent down the floors. All I knew was that I needed to do was to keep moving otherwise the ceiling tile would give out, and I would be compromised.

Too late. Me just thinking about the worst outcome, gave me the worst possibility. The sneeze was eminent now. As I let go of holding it in, a gust of wind let out of me that was a king among other sneezes. Other sneezes would have bowed before this one. Well, the bad news was, it was loud and it forced a crack in the ceiling tile and it clamored to the floor. A man with slick black hair stared up at me after seeing the mess. "Why you shouldn't be up there kiddo. Come on down. I'll help you out."

At this point I didn't have much of a choice so I let go of the pipe holding me up there. I dropped to the floor with a thud. I landed square on my back and struggled to get up. The man looked me in the eyes and said, "Come on Kyle, time to get up."

What's odd is that his eyes were a light shade of purple. And as you would look into them, with his voice as well, like a hypnotic rhythm.

I stood up instinctively as my actions followed his voice. "So kid, why are you snooping around these parts of the Legion's buildings?"

The last thing I wanted to do was admit I was spying on Joey, but my lips defied me. "We were in the ventilation system watching our friend, Joey's meeting. Or at least trying to. We couldn't hear or see anyone other than Joey."

The mans fist pounded against the desk he stood behind. The cup of coffee that sat on the desk was now tipped on its side spewing out the coffee that once belonged to someone. The nameplate on the desk read "Morpheus." Wait Morpheus! Purple hypnotic eyes. He had me sleep talking. That was Morpheus, God of Dreams.

I couldn't speak up now. If I did he would know who I really was. For now, all he had admitted that my name was Kyle. If he found out I had heard what these people were up to, Morpheus would kill me on the spot. Now it was up for me to come up with a clever escape plan, or for Brian to pull a rescue stunt. Either option would be a horrible idea, but it was all I had to hope for.

"Look kid, if you're lost say so. The guards will kindly lead you on your way. Unless you have something else you are here for?" His head made a motion behind him. In a large picture frame was a symbol. I had seen it before. A skull with a dagger through it. I had seen this symbol throughout people within Demigod Central before, including Joey.

Morpheus took a seat on top of his desk and crossed his legs. He began to smile intently. He must have enjoyed seeing the panic come across my face. "What is that a picture of?" I asked in almost terror.

Morpheus smiled sinisterly at me, "What do you fear it may be child?"

My eye twitched in recognition of where I now was. That was the symbol for the Legion of Tartarus. Joey was here to talk with them. He left me and Brian outside so we wouldn't find out. Joey was going to sell us out and join them.

"Suspicion grows on those who do not speak child? Do you have something to hide from me son of the sea?"

"What did you just call me?" I asked in alarm.

He chuckled slightly. In his hands appeared a clay that kept shifting into different shapes. At one point I saw a wolf, the next a whale, and then a human. Just as quickly as the human appeared it was squashed back into nothingness. "I called you by a title of yours Kyle. Kyle Pierce, I believe it is. Son of Poseidon. The alleged receiver of a horribly great fate. Tasked to save the Realms and everything that inhabits them. Oh what horror and pains that will be brought to you."

Morpheus knew he had found a nerve to pick. He smirked after each dig he got in. My bewildered face began to fill with rage. My slack hand began to clench into a fist. The waves inside me went from being a calm beach to a raging hurricane.

Just as I thought I might do something rash, the phone on his desk rang. My fist subtly unclenched a bit, but I was still on guard. He picked up the phone with such ease, as though our tension was nonexistent. "Yello," he said cheerfully and eagerly.

He paused momentarily listening to the other end of the call. "Well, yes we need that. And what do you mean there are pigs labeled 1, 3, and 4 running around? Have you found the one labeled 2? Hold on I will be right down." He slammed the phone back down on the receiver. "You don't move away from my desk Kyle. I will be right back."

He got up and walked out of the room in a quickened pace and then sprinted down the stair case.

I sat there momentarily then realized this was the escape I was waiting for. Brian had pulled off a successful distraction. I hoisted myself out of the chair and began to sprint down the hall. Halfway down the hall I saw a familiar face. My mentor, Loki.

I froze in fear, was he with us or against us? Then the elevator dinged. Out of the elevator sprung my spunky little archer buddy, Brian. He had his bow strung and ready to open fire. "Took you long enough," Loki chimed at him.

"I'm sorry I can't teleport like you can Loki."

I stared at the two arguing. Loki finally turned upon seeing me and outstretched his arms, "Ah Kyle! My young little demigod pupil, that I am being forced to watch out for!"

"That's very reassuring to hear Loki, but why are you here?" And I thought about how he had said forced. I was really questioning this god's intentions. I was almost curious to have Loki sit and wait for Morpheus to come back, and let him have him. Those two would have such a splendid talk. Or pull one another's slicked backed greased hair out.

"I'm here because I am your mentor, and time calls for an escape. I'm sure you heard the call from the guard. I changed up the simple antics of mine. I changed the 2 to a 3. Throws them off every time. Threw you all into madness for a few hours back in Kansas years ago. However, these people are better trained, and there is about fifteen times more of them than there were you back in those lonely fields of Kansas." Loki had looked so pleased with himself. I didn't want to burst his bubble that Morpheus was probably onto the trick, but I feel as though Loki was much like the Greek goddess Tyche and just full of luck.

I had met Tyche's, Roman counterpart Fortuna, and she had a whole opera house singing "O Fortuna" just for her. It was kind of awkward. But the goddess had made calculations for everything, but luck was always her favorite calculation. I feared that Loki was similar to her, or causing chaos. Whichever suited this deranged god better.

He interlaced his fingers, "Now young half-bloods, we need to get out of this building. Anything that is labeled Tartarus strikes me with a bad taste in my mouth. Similar to that of gasoline. I'd rather spend time with and in Hel than with or in Tartarus. And Hel is a pretty bad place as is." Loki spattered as if he were actually tasting gasoline.

CHAPTER 19

AN ARROW TO THE HEAD

Loki flung his wrist and the fire button lit up on the elevator. "I'm forgetting something," he said frantically tapping his finger on his forehead. "Ah yes!" he exclaimed. He rushed to the table and scribbled something on a sticky note.

Now, I wish I could tell you we did something epic, but no. We didn't do anything of the sorts. Loki just grabbed Brian and my shoulder and teleported us into the car. I may have screamed a little bit, but who am I to say.

Loki sat in the back seat of the car and looked at me. "I know I have given you reason to doubt me, but trust me Kyle, I will help you when time comes. I know I am not the best. I am not an evil deity. I have done wrong, but I feel as though amends hold a greater value in the long run. Grudges cannot be held forever, and I hope one day Thor and the other gods can see of such. One last piece of advice that I can give to help you on you quest. Seek out the red headed girl. She has a great knowledge and likes certain facts of Presidents whom have been assassinated. Now I must return to my castle. My daughter Hel is coming over for tea, and butterscotch crumpets."

"Crumpets?" Brian asked.

"Yes, they are quite tasty." With that Loki had disappeared.

Brian turned around with a confused look on his face, "Wait Hel is his daughter? And does that mean he would actually want to spend time with Tartarus?"

I gave Brian one of those looks when you know he had just said something absolutely stupid. "Brian, just shut up. Loki saved us, so let's not mention it to Joey."

"Yeah, that sounds like a plan," he said as he slouched back in his seat and turned on the radio.

Joey walked over to car and slammed the door shut behind him. We could sense that he was in a bitter mood. He shut off the radio, and with that began Brian's complaining.

"I was listening to that!" He whined.

"Not now," Joey commanded while furiously reversing the car. I held onto the side hoping I would not be whipped around.

He sped up and rammed through the gate. Once he had gotten us back onto the highway he began to talk to us again. "Care to tell me why the alarm went off in there?"

"In where?" I asked.

"Don't play this game Kyle. Why was the building's intruder alarm going off? I know you two did something. At least Brian did."

Brian turned to Joey and punched him in the face. "Why didn't you tell me you were working with them again?"

"Hey!" I said in a concerned matter. "Let's not crash the car."

Joey laughed, "No that is a great idea, how about I do crash the car." He began to dangerously swerve in and out of the lanes cutting other drivers off and nearly missing a tractor trailer.

Brian drew an arrow, "Don't make me put one in your skull, Joey."

"Do it!" Joey yelled as he pulled the steering wheel all the way to the left, veering us across traffic. The car flipped twice, and got broadsided into the cement barrier.

Upon opening my eyes, I could see glass shattered everywhere. I was hanging upside down, still buckled in. As I unclipped my seatbelt I dropped to the floor banging my head. "Ugh," I moaned. Joey was already out of the car walking. Blood trickled down his forehead from a cut above his eyebrow.

Brian stumbled out of the car kicking his door off of it's hinge. "What the hell Joey! Yeah, we broke in there to find out what was going on. But you, you have been working with them for years. When we found Demigod Central, you said you were done. That you had changed. You have been still working with them, this whole time!" Brian had an arrow notched and was five feet away from Joey. "Why should I not put this arrow in you right now?"

I slid myself out of the car watching the horror of Brian confronting Joey, and the realization that Joey was a member of the Legion all along.

Joey looked at Brian with a remorseful look in his eyes, "Go ahead. Do it. End what I have begun in vein. Yeah, I started out working with the Legion of Tartarus in order to protect you Brian. They provided us safety, and in return I would complete tasks for them. We were hitmen for a while. Those who were against the Legion, we either turned them to our side or took them down."

Brian was tearing up and screamed at him, "LIAR!"

Joey knelt to the ground, laced his fingers together and placed them behind his head. "Go ahead, I deserve whatever punishment you see fit, Brian. I did it to protect you when we were on our own, and I just paid my last debt I owed to them. So now all I have to do with the Legion, is this damn tattoo on my arm. That's why I started the Bunker. As a safe place from the Legion, but I realized that with me there that isn't true. That's what my desire was that the Kapre showed me, to eradicate myself from the grips of the Legion once and for all. If you can forgive me I'd like to finish our quest."

I had managed to get behind Brian and place my hand on his shoulder. "This is not worth it Brian. He is your brother. Save your rage for the monsters we may face. We are almost to D.C. now. I am certain we could find a tour group to get us closer since our car is now totaled."

Brian let his bow go slack. He lowered it and put his arrow back into his quiver. He walked over to Joey and gave him a hug. I could see the pain in his eyes as they watered up.

I called a taxi on my phone and within twenty minutes we were on the road once more. In hindsight we probably should have dealt with the messed up car instead of leaving it on the side of the road to clog up traffic. But c'mon traffic in the Washington D.C. area cannot possibly be that bad?

CHAPTER 20

NIGHTBOW AND THE QUEST FOR MONEY

Turns out traffic was just that, bad. Truly awful. As I looked out the taxi window and to the sky, the sun had disappeared and stuck behind the clouds. The lack of the sun in the afternoon sky was kind of upsetting.

"This is as far as I will go with your money. You're out now," the cabbie said.

Joey fished out $12.73 and handed it to him as we got out of the car.

"Be grateful guys, at least you're near the Metro now." The cabbie sped off and left us on the curbside.

I looked at the cab driver as he pulled away. Brian still was not talking to Joey. But he was beginning to forgive his brother some. Which was a start.

Joey looked around. "How do you guys plan to getting to wherever it is we need to go? Do we even know where?"

Brian scratched his head trying to think. "Lincoln Memorial," I said swiftly.

"Where did you get that idea?" Joey asked confused. It was time I mentioned Loki coming to my aid.

"Loki told us."

Joey chuckled, "Oh that's great. Loki? We are going to listen to him now? What did he do back in Kansas!" Joey was serious about not wanting to trust Loki.

Brian kicked his feet against the dirt. "Loki saved us from the Legion of Tartarus' office building. And then he gave us a bit of advice after getting us out of there. He mentioned that we'd find some girl who likes a President, who was assassinated. And well, Lincoln was a President of the United States."

"It's the only lead we've got," I said. "We gotta get there somehow." I pulled out my phone and opened its maps application. "According to this it's roughly an hour walk with the subway stopping every so often."

Joey looked around, and then pointed to a sign on the sidewalk with an M on it. "Their subway system is called the Metro, and they also have a bus service. Now we just need some money."

Nothing was around us, except for an old soccer stadium. And the sidewalk where we could wait for the bus.

"Aha!" Brian quickly said as he put on his mask and shot an arrow at the stadium.

"Brian what are you doing?" Joey quickly asked in

confusion.

"Getting us some money. I'll be back." He had tied a rope to his arrow and launched himself into the air and into the stadium.

Joey and myself sat in silence poking at the dirt and loose rocks on the curb.

He decided to break the silence, "So Loki saved you all back there then. And he was genuinely concerned for your all's safety?"

I nodded, "Yes, he was sincere. He says he wants respect like he used to get. I mean it makes sense. If we truly are special, he'd want to protect us."

Joey teetered his head. "I guess that makes sense. I still don't like him, but I appreciate the fact that he helped you two. Do you think we will find the book?"

His voice seemed to know something and it sounded like it was leading to something. I froze in silence. Then I thought about my dream, I had seen Chrysaor and Vivian planning something. They had the book, but they also said they needed to set something up.

"I think we can pull something off and manage to find it," I stated positively.

Just then Brian had dropped from a zip line in front of us. "Did anybody need some bus money?" He said ripping off his mask. He opened up his bag and showed over $30 in coins alone. Let alone all the bills he had acquired.

"Well, looks like we don't need to sneak onto the Metro anymore," Joey said surprised. "Way to go Nightbow."

We waited at the bus stop for about five minutes and finally a bus arrived heading for the National Mall. Perfect.

The three of us boarded the bus and found seats in the back of the bus. We looked out the window and enjoyed the sights. I began to realize that the beginning of the end of our quest was finally going to begin.

CHAPTER 21

THE TOURIST

We stepped off the Metro bus and looked at the National Mall. Washington D.C. was nothing like it was in the history books they had at Demigod Central. The Washington Monument reminded me of the Palladium Chiron had once showed me that protected all of mythologies in existence. Without the Palladium the mythical creatures could die for good, and this included the gods as well. The Palladium was the most important thing in all of the Realms, but only Chiron knew its true location.

We saw a tour group ahead and Brian looked at Joey, "We should join in with the tour. If we are going to find this Book of Whatever then some tour guide might mention some clue, we could use to locate it."

Joey contemplated the idea. The 22-year-old sat there with two 16-year-olds lost in D.C. Another tour group passed us heading towards the Lincoln Memorial. There was a redheaded girl in the group that just kept arguing with the tour guide. "You said Lincoln was killed by a bullet wound to the front of his head. Booth snuck into the box Lincoln was in and shot him in the back of his head."

I looked at the rest of the group. "Well, I don't know about you all but I found the group I am going with. This girl will probably know something." The other two agreed in unison and we walked into the tour group picking up an info map from a stand we passed on the street. Joey studied the pamphlet while Brian and myself paid close attention to the tour guide and this girl and her bickering.

We began to walk up the steps of the Lincoln Memorial and the guide began to say, "President Lincoln stood on these steps as he delivered the," he paused down and looked at a fact card he had on hand. "The Gettysburg Address!"

The girl lost it and ran up to a step higher than the tour guide to look him in the eyes. "*WRONG! WRONG! WRONG!*" she screamed in his face. "The Lincoln Memorial was not built while he was in office! It began construction in 1914 and was finished in 1922. He gave the Gettysburg Address on November 19, 1863, in Gettysburg! For a tour guide you know nothing!"

The tour guides face was almost as red as the girl's hair. The girl looked to be about our age as well. Brian looked at me, "Maybe a daughter of Athena based on her intelligence."

I smirked back at him, "Maybe Minerva is a closer guess seeing her warlike nature."

"Aw dude, just cause she's a ginger don't go saying they are rash and tend to fight."

"It's true."

"Yeah, I know. I try to forget about it though."

A familiar voice chided behind me, "You know she is pretty smart for a daughter of Athena."

I spun around recognizing whose voice, it belonged to, Gwen! I gave her a huge bear hug. After releasing her from the hug I looked her in the eyes, "What are you doing here? Who's watching the Bunker?"

At this point Joey had rejoined us, showing concern himself. "No one is watching the Bunker. The twins are with Nicole. She's pretty neat actually."

Brian perked up momentarily, "Nicole? Who in Hades name is she? Wait, is she the new girl who doesn't like me?"

Gwen chuckled, "Well a daughter of Hades actually, and yes." Unknowingly I tensed up. It was like some natural rivalry between me and any other kid of Zeus or Hades. I still did not like her from my little rooftop encounter with her.

I looked back towards the bickering going on at the top of the Lincoln Memorial.

The tour guide stared at this girl. "Who do you think you are telling me what is right and wrong about history?"

She perked up and did a classic Peter Pan pose by putting her fists upon her hips with her arms bowed. "My name is

Miranda Callaghan! And yes, you know nothing regarding Lincoln, and quite frankly most history. You won't win in a history competition against me."

The tour guide ripped off the sash around his chest. "You know what Miss Callaghan!"

"What?" she interrupted sarcastically.

"I quit!" he said as he stormed down the steps cursing and muttering about some dumb red head ruining his life.

"And that folks, is how you give proper history facts. No one messes with my favorite President and gets away with it." She bowed as if she had just put on a show.

Brian clapped slowly in amazement. Joey covered his face with his palm laughing at Brian's reaction to the girl who had just proved the former guide wrong. The girl notched an eyebrow and looked at us in a confused manner. She began to walk towards us down the steps.

"Act calm everyone," Brian said nervously.

Joey retorted saying, "Ha! The only one not calm is you little bro. Just be yourself."

Miranda was now in front of us now. Her smile was radiant. Her red hair was astonishing as it radiated the beams of light from the sun making it appear gold. It was wavy and long, but still amazing. She was about 5'9". All around she was beautiful. She was probably one of it not the prettiest girl I had ever seen. Now I understood why Brian was acting that way. Aphrodite herself would be jealous of her.

"Your jaws open. You might catch a few flies leaving them open a little bit longer. My name is Miranda Callaghan. Nice to meet you all." She turned towards Gwen, "And I see you've caught back up."

Me and Brian adjusted our gaze into a less awkward stare. But she had already noticed it.

Joey spoke up and spoke softly trying to ease the conversation, "Hi I am Joey Schmitz and this here is my brother Brian. And this is his best friend Kyle Pierce."

She nodded her head in understanding. She began to size us up and I began to reach for my sword hidden in my backpack. "You three are demigods like myself. We got a son of the sea and two sons of the sun. *Bam!*"

We looked at one another in awe. She had just guess are lineage with ease. If a half-blood could do this did that mean monsters would sense us as well?

"How do you know that we are demigods?" I asked flustered. "*Erh*, what makes you think demigods are even real?"

She rolled her eyes at me, "Idiot. I'm a daughter of Athena. I am not stupid. I can also tell your backpack is not a backpack but a magical sheath hiding a 4-foot-long two-handed sword. Made out of some eerie black metal. And

Brian here has got bow that turns into dual swords under his coat. If you three wanna pretend you are not demigods can you at least act the role of a tourist. Besides, Gwen already found me and informed me of you three."

Now Joey's mouth was hung open awe struck. No one ever talked to him like that. Something told me that this girl would eventually get frustrated with us. But something told me whatever would cause it she would not hold a grudge. And I hoped that my hunch was right. If this held true she would be a great asset.

She looked at us, "So what are you all looking for anyways? Some monster? Some magical sword? I've helped plenty of demigods searching for stuff in my days. Even some computer hacker recently on how to find some corporate building for some file for an upcoming job."

Joey guessed she could be of use and finally said, "You ever hear of Athena's book collection. Two of her most important books, The Book of Wisdom and The Book of Shadows, well both of them are gone."

"Book of Shadows? That's an easy one! It's in the Library of Congress. It's just sitting in one of the back shelves."

Her red hair blew against the wind crashing into her face. The colors in her hair were like flames dancing across a fire in the hearth. I then thought how the wind had an odd warmth too it that had just messed up Miranda's hair. Wait why am I focusing on her hair? *Get a grip on yourself*, I thought

161

to myself.

I glanced at Gwen and tried to keep focus on her. This Miranda was just captivating though, and it seemed Gwen had noticed my sudden interest in her.

Across the street was a man in a midnight black suit and had his hair slicked back like he was a hockey player. He just stared intently at the five of us without saying a word. It was really creepy if you ask me about it. But, I recognized the creepiness instantly, Morpheus. He had followed us after the break in.

Joey turned towards him and said, "I'll be back guys. Looks like we have a god watching us. Take a selfie or something. We are almost done this quest."

Miranda pulled out Brian's phone and took a group picture. "There," she remarked.

"Good," he smirked as he jogged across the street and met with the god. They both shook hands and began to joke like they were old friends. This didn't make any sense. I turned to Brian and he stared intently at his brother conversing with a demigods' worst nightmare.

"Do you know why he is talking to Morpheus now?" I asked hoping he would have any insight on it.

"No idea. I thought he said he was done with the Legion and that's how he got out of getting an arrow to the head."

Miranda rolled her eyes at us and began to scold us. "You

two are idiots. Why is the God of Dreams here? This monster, he bends peoples dreams into showing their deepest fears. He also messes with your life too. He's like the Greek version of Loki."

"I know that's who it was. I was trying to get Brian to know what they are talking about. I ran into him when I was in the Legion's building. How do you know who he is?" I asked Miranda in confusion.

She looked down at her feet not making eye contact. I had entered a touchy subject without even realizing it. "He came to me a few years ago with an offer to join some team *they* were forming."

Brian perked up at hearing "they." He stammered, "*They*? Who are *they*?"

"I don't know," she murmured in a sadden voice. Miranda said it as though she were holding back anger and pain. From what I was seeing she was strong and independent, but she needed someone to help be her crutch from time to time. "But when I rejected his offer he showed me my dad dying. I thought it was merely a dream, but he had already put it into action. I came home to find my dad dead, and my mother, Athena, was there. She, she just looked at me shaking her head telling me I had done the right thing."

Without thinking about it I gave her a hug. She wanted to punch me and she was frustrated that I had given her a hug, but she didn't push me away either. I could feel the icy stare coming from Gwen. I needed to talk to her.

"So this Morpheus guy is a real ass-wipe then?" Brian asked still staring at his brother. I was wondering what Morpheus was showing Joey. We had all assumed he was being given an offer similar to Miranda's. In fact, I knew these two had conversed before. He was probably reassuring the deal even though Joey claims he was leaving that life behind.

Miranda chuckled as she wiped a tear from her eye, "Yeah. I wish I had the courage to go over there and just have him know the pain he put me through."

A low deep raspy voice spoke behind us, "Payback may sound like a good idea, but in reality what does it accomplish? Nothing. It only worsens a situation furthering the rift between the two." The four of us turned to see a 7-foot-tall knight in golden armor behind us, Chrysaor! "Look I'll be blunt about this whole situation, where's the damn book?" he asked.

CHAPTER 22

CHRYSAOR GOES FOR A SWIM

It was a trap and he was here for the book as well. But didn't he have the book originally? My breath became heavy with panic. I was supposed to know what to do in this situation, but I had just frozen in fear instead.

The man just stood there. His dark skin glinted through his golden armor. Chrysaor, the son of Poseidon and the blood of Medusa, my half-brother. And it was time I fought the monster once solely hell bent on killing Perseus.

I tried to think on what I could do but my mind was blank. Fight or flight had to kick in eventually, right?

Finally, after standing there motionless for a few moments, my mind decided to finally turn on. I began to run the options through my mind. *Fight?* No way, too risky especially in the open. *Run?* Seems like it was our only option. So naturally I said, "Bare with me for a second. Just let me tie my shoe and get you that."

I had picked up a rock and chucked it right at his metal helmet. One of the horns on his helmet snapped right off and clattered to the floor.

"*RUN!*" I screamed, and naturally no one had any objections to that.

Gwen, lucky for me, was using her power of plants. She was using all of the surrounding vegetation to make it hard for Chrysaor to get by.

We sprinted down the Vietnam Memorial Wall and I had almost knocked over a veteran if I didn't roll out of the way. In doing so, I had rolled into a thorn bush. Fine with me just as long as I didn't see the golden hunk of metal chasing me. Too late. He swung his giant sword and it pounded the ground at my feet. I scrambled backwards and completely ignored the thorns or anything. This was now about survival.

I had lost sight of Joey, Brian, Gwen, and Miranda but they knew where to go. I just needed to keep Chrysaor distracted. I could feel in my gut a smaller body of water, but it wasn't the Potomac or the reflecting pool, it was some sort of pond. I didn't know why but I figured I could stand a chance fighting with water on my side even if he was also a son of Poseidon.

I scrambled to my feet and sprinted around the Golden One. He was quick, and obviously skilled with his sword, but I needed something more than instinct. I did need to survive, but I needed to protect others as well.

I sprinted along the path in hopes of finding this pond that was somewhere nearby. *C'mon*, I thought to myself as I continued sprinting. There was too much of a crowd around me to do anything.

I ducked past a hot dog vendor and drew my sword Shadow. "Hey get out of the way!" I screamed at a crowd of people in my area. It was probably the stupidest thing I could do at the time too. I pictured the news headline for the evening news being, "*Crazed Teen With Sword Threatens Tourists In D.C.*" Yeah that'd be a great headline, followed by some video that the tourists were getting on their smartphones.

A father and son almost ran into me. The son looked at me and could tell a sword was in my hand. I stared at him confused and forgot momentarily why I was running.

"Sword," the kid said.

"Hunh?" I asked confused. Then it hit me. No like it literally hit me, like a baseball bat. The blunt side of Chrysaor's sword caught me and sent me flying to the edge of the pond. I let out a grunt and tried to pull myself to the water.

I had lost Shadow somewhere back by the kid. That dang kid had to have been a demigod. No way he would tell me that I had a sword with such a straight face. I tried to regain my focus. Shadow would reappear in my backpack shortly. I just needed to get to the water. I reached my hand out to touch the surface of the water and I took a hard blow to the side of my ribs. I had gotten pushed further away from the pond.

The blow was like nothing I had ever taken in training. This was not some training dummy that would get shut off before it would hurt me. This was real life and he was really out to kill me. I pushed myself up to a knee and he came over just to lift up his knee quickly launching me into the pond.

As I sunk beneath the water everything was in pain. My insides burned in a scorching pain. My face had a cut on it above my left eyebrow. I breathed in when I hit the bottom of the pond and sat upright. The water was giving me a will to fight.

My eyes jolted open and I swam to the surface. I hopped onto the little island's memorial and realized exactly where I was. Constitution Gardens Pond. And I was now standing on the 56 Signers of the Declaration of Independence Memorial.

I had now regained my strength and as Chrysaor waded through the water, I sprinted across the bridge and towards the Washington Monument. I needed to get to the Library of Congress and meet up with the others fast. I spun around to face Chrysaor and flung my hand towards the water, forming a wall of water. As I began to concentrate I yelled, "*FREEZE!*"

To my astonishment, it had worked and I had just controlled ice. Or water into ice. How had I finally done it?

I sprinted towards the Washington Monument to try to get a bearing of which direction I needed to head towards, and then I heard the ear piercing noise. I spun around and saw the wall of ice come tumbling down. He had broken right through it. *Great,* I thought, *I'm never going to lose this guy.* I then continued my sprinting until I finally made it to where I could see the Capitol. Ok. Now the Library of Congress was somewhere around there. I hope.

I ran towards the Smithsonian's. I needed to lose this guy somewhere.

I felt the early spring sun glaze against my skin. I stopped and admired the warmth, until a glare formed in my eyes. What was it from? Wait, was that from Chrysaor?

Turns out, it was him. His sword clashed in front of me, impaling my jacket. "A true shame brother. I was hoping for a real challenge like the old days. I used to enjoy slaughtering foes who dared take me on in the ring. Gladiator matches were the best. What do you say you just bring me to the book and I let you and your friends live?"

I pondered the thought. If we just let him have it, we could walk free. At least I had hoped this was the case. However, I couldn't be sure. I needed to make sure this new girl, Miranda stayed out of harms way. And especially Gwen. I wasn't going to let anything happen to her. And if Chrysaor did anything to Brian or Joey, I wouldn't be able to live with myself. But I couldn't risk this quest. All I needed was some more time for a plan, or something to form in my mind.

All of the sudden an arrow landed in between me and my half-brother. "What's this?" he said quizzically. As he bent down to pick it up it combusted in his hand followed by a small explosion. Brian had rigged an arrow to blow up on touch. Clever.

I ripped my jacket free from Chrysaor's swords grasp. I ran towards Brian as he volleyed another arrow towards him. "Let's go Kyle! Come on!"

As I caught up with him we sprinted towards the Capitol and saw security go nuts. Joey, Gwen, and Miranda went around, and well to save time we naturally ran through it. Why waste the time going around when you can go through something? Like really, some common sense at times helps a lot.

At least I can say it was a good idea until the metal detector went off. Within seconds Capitol Hill Police officers were on alert of us.

"Up?" I asked cautiously.

We both quickly glanced up and saw officers with their rifles pointed towards us. "Nope!" Brian retorted in an urgent pace. He looked towards the window. "There!" We ran towards it and he smashed it with his bow. He climbed out onto the ledge and propelled down after securing a line. I followed him and instantly grew skittish.

"Uhm," I paused as I grew shaky against the ledge. "A tad bit scared of heights," I admitted. Just then a gun fired, and the bullet nearly hit me in the shoulder. I jumped and grabbed the rope without further hesitation.

We ran across the street and somehow avoided the officers and closed the doors behind us relieved to see Joey, Gwen, and Miranda in here already. Too close for comfort in my mind.

CHAPTER 23

THE NOT SO QUIET LIBRARY OF OUR END

I slumped against the door and was catching my breath. I closed my eyes and recounted what I had just done. I had just ran from my half-brother and somehow evaded him. I breathed in heavily and then my breathing began to refocus. I opened my eyes and saw Brian pulling me to my feet. Miranda began to search through the aisles looking for the book. Joey began to clear everyone out of the back door after he set a table on fire.

"We need to barricade the doors fast. He is gonna find us here if he hasn't already tracked us to this location," Brian stated with urgency.

"I'm already ahead of you on securing the building Brian." Gwen was occupied with summoning vines and tying up all of the doors.

Joey had just extinguished the fire he had made to scare out the innocent civilians. "If he doesn't find us I'm certain either the police or fire department will be here first."

Miranda frantically pulled out books. She began to throw

the books that were not what she wanted across the room. "Guys, I swear to you all that the Book of Shadows was here last week. But it isn't here anymore. If the Legion of Tartarus doesn't have it, and we are looking for it as well. Then who has it?"

Brian and myself walked towards Miranda. She was on the verge of pulling her hair out in frustration. She began to pace the room angrily. "How is it not here!"

"Maybe someone else already found it?" I asked in confusion.

"The book can only be opened by children of Athens! The inside said that it could only be them! Who else could have it?"

I began to shake my head in disgust. "You do know children of Athens refers to children of Greece. Chrysaor is technically my brother, a fellow Greek."

"No, but the book was here. I swear to you." I felt bad for Miranda. She truly was trying to help us now, but there wasn't much she could do.

Gwen walked over and put her arm around Miranda. "Hey look at me," she said calmly. "Look at me." Miranda looked up a bit teary eyed. "Hey, we will find you that book. And you're gonna be part of this."

Joey walked up to her, "Welcome to Bunker 4921."

Brian leaned against the bookcase, "I still say we should

get jackets. Everybody loves a nice jacket."

Miranda was beginning to smile at Brian's comment. However, her happiness was short lived.

There were three slow claps from the center of the library. Chrysaor stood on the center desk clapping. "Demigods! Half-Bloods! Little shits! Or whatever you all wanna be called. Welcome to your demise."

The five of us stood in silence. I knew Joey had enough energy left to summon a Realm portal for maybe half a moment. The last of his emergency tie in with Hermes.

Hermes gave it him as payment for a quest he did a few years back. Joey had used it from time to time, but this would be the last of it. And it would only last for a few seconds.

Brian and myself looked at him anxiously. "Joey you are going to have to use it. We can't beat him. Not now. It would be physically impossible for us to do so." Brian was close to begging.

I lowered my head and glanced towards the first floor. I could see the tip of his helmet and his broken horn out there. "Get the girls out of here. I'm going to go settle this."

Gwen looked at me, "Kyle don't! It'll be suicide doing it."

"I know. But you all need to get to safety. Alert Akhbar and Chiron that the Book of Shadows is no longer here. I'm going to go settle this with my brother."

Gwen rushed forward in a surge of emotion and hugged me. Her lip was quivering. "Don't do it. Just leave with us. Come on Kyle! Please!"

"Gwen," I tried to plead. "If I don't stop him here. He will continue to let the Legion of Tartarus grow." I said this as I gave Joey a stern look. "If we let the Legion continue to run amok then it's game over for us. Everything we have learned at Demigod Central would mean nothing, and they will ruin the Realms."

Brian still leaned against the book case rubbing his shoulder. "Well Kyle, if this is the case. We are partners till the end man. I'm sticking with you. Joey, I am asking this brother to brother. Get Miranda and Gwen back to Demigod Central to safety."

Joey shook his head with a smug smirk on his face, "You two may be the stupidest brave duo I've ever known. I'll see you on the other side."

With that he opened the portal and he stared at it for a few moments. Miranda gave Brian and myself a quick hug. Gwen did not want to let go of me.

"Gwen c'mon go! Please!"

"I'm not leaving you! Not this time."

"I did say partners till then end Kyle. And they are partners." Brian was smiling knowing this would not end well for us most likely.

Joey looked at the portal once more and let it close. He smiled at us and I smiled back at him and the others too. "Alright," I said cocky, "let's go whoop some Chrysaor butt!"

I heard Chrysaor yell in rage, "Show yourself you cowards."

I could tell his patience was wearing thin. Luckily for me I had a plan. Yeah that's right, I had my own plan. Not going to rely on Loki to bail me out, not again. He was my mentor for a reason, and at this moment it was for me to figure my way out of something. I had learned my lesson back in Morpheus' Office.

I huddled the rest of Bunker 4921 into a huddle. "Ok guys," I started and quickly told Brian and Gwen what I needed them to do. I did the same for for Miranda and Joey in order for this to truly work.

I walked to the ledge overlooking the center. "Yeah fat face I'm on my way."

I could see a smile creep across his face, "About time brother. I fear you had coward away from a fight. You and me have an unsettled score. I think we put it to an end."

"I couldn't agree more."

"You know I would've settled for you just giving me the Book of Shadows, right."

"I know. But I figured you could use the exercise."

"Got any more insults or can I just pry this book off of your dead corpse yet."

I pondered the thought. Maybe I should've taken up this guys offer to let them walk originally. But there was a small issue, actually quite a rather large one. I didn't have the book.

I glanced and finally got a true look at his mismatch of armor. The armor itself was like some kindergartener's collage of cut out pictures from a magazine then glue to an undersized poster board. I noticed his helmet was some cross over style between the gladiator's of Rome and a Viking horned helmet. His breastplate was a mix of Greek and Roman. He wore a medieval style knight gauntlet on one arm and the other had a cuff on it. He wore a Greek infantry skirt, which was metal plated instead of leather, odd. His shin pads, well those, I had no idea personally.

After a quick assessment of his armor, I was chalking it up as those were his spoils of war. His personal trophies and warning sign to his enemies. That he was a force not be reckoned with.

I finally was brave enough to challenge the Golden One. I just hoped that Gwen and Brian were in place by now. I only had one shot at taking him down and it would have to be done. I leaped the edge and was now thirty feet in front of my worst nightmare. A sword yielding maniac.

I clenched my left fist while I shifted the weight of Shadow in my right hand. It felt perfectly balanced now. It seemed to have an understanding that this was a dire situation.

"So Kyle, where's this Book of Shadows?" He rubbed the broken horn on his helmet. I could see resentment in the darken eyeholes of his helmet. He seemed to notice my fear, "You know I am history's greatest gladiator for a reason. I knew how to win. I was and still am ruthless. And I'm damn sure not going to lose to you."

"It's not here!" I said sternly. I was not going to let him intimidate me. Not now. I was not going to give him anymore satisfaction.

Out of the corner of my eyes I noticed Brian had somehow managed to perch himself where I needed him to be. Now only for Gwen to get into place. Too bad I did not have the time to check, because the battle had begun.

Shadow intercepted the 4-foot-long blade and sparks flew. "Hmm," he chided. "You don't have any armor to add to my collection. I could use a new blade though."

C'mon Gwen, I thought. I needed to know if she was in place before I'd start the offensive attack.

He swung his blade again. Again Shadow intercepted it, but not with the same integrity. My strength began to wane and my sword balance faltered. Chrysaor's blade came down on my arm leaving a good size gash.

He continued to pursue his assault. He grazed my left leg and I crumpled to the floor in pain. Shadow clattered to the floor.

Chrysaor walked over and put his boot on my chest, "Nothing personal. Just business." He readied his sword for the kill.

Just then an arrow whizzed into Chrysaor's exposed chest. Brian had managed to knick him right in a chink in the armor. He looked at the arrow and pulled it out without a hitch.

However, upon pulling it out he realized the mistake. "Go figure. The bow of Heracles fired an arrow with the blood of the Lernaean Hydra. Typical half-blood move."

He backpedaled and fell over a vine. Gwen had managed to lace the floor with vines. But she wasn't finished and Chrysaor stood up yanking at the vine. He reeled Gwen in and held her by her ankle. He violently twisted her ankle, sending a bone chilling noise as it snapped.

My heart sank. He had hurt Gwen. I rushed towards Shadow and sprinted, or limped towards the Golden One. I impaled his upper thigh with Shadow. He howled in pain and dropped Gwen on her head.

Chrysaor's sword clanked to the ground. "See your friends did not need to get involved Kyle. This is all your fault."

"No Chrysaor, it's yours. You think you are the best warrior in the world. You have an issue with pride. But today, you have met your match."

He smiled through his helmet. "You think so. You think that you and your friends, the Demigod Trio, can beat me? Son of Poseidon and Medusa. What do you have a son of Poseidon, that fails to see his potential. A son of Wi, the forgotten god. And a tree hugging daughter of Demeter. You are nothing."

I shook my head making an advance on him. "We are not nothing. We aren't the Demigod Trio either. We are heroes. Heroes of Bunker 4921. That's what we are. And we don't whim to monsters."

"Well kid, you are in for a good wake up call then. When you actually have to face the Legion of Tartarus, and it's might, you will fall."

I pulled Shadow out of Chrysaor's leg and impaled the other. I swiftly yanked it back out and he fell to his knees. I pointed the blade at his heart. Although it was still protected by his breastplate I was showing that I meant business.

"Leave us alone at once! Never return and I'll let you live."

Brian began to climb down off of the scaffolding he perched himself on. Chrysaor looked intently into my eyes. Even though I could not see his visibly, they concentrated long and hard on me.

"You're the wrong one," he said softly and confused.

"What?" I said in confusion. "Speak up. I couldn't hear you."

He looked back up and smiled, "You're the wrong one. You are not the one who can stop us. I'm no longer needed here then."

Brian jogged towards me, "What is he saying?"

"Goodbye half-bloods. Until we meet again. And as one of you knows the only way I am to die." Chrysaor grabbed his neck and snapped it right in front of us.

His body fell lifeless, in a crumpled heap. What once stood as a 7-foot-tall giant adversary now lay dead in front of us. More scarily he had looked directly at me when saying it. It was like Perseus had said dying in Chrysaor's arms, he could only die by his neck. But apparently it didn't need to be severed.

Gwen began to pull herself up limping as Brian helped her.

I stared aimlessly at the dead body. My half-brother, he had just told me I was the wrong one. The wrong one for what? He came to this realization and just decided to kill himself?

Brian walked up to the helmet of Chrysaor and snapped the other horn off of his helmet. "You never know when this might come in handy. It's always good to have a sidearm if anything ever becomes too serious."

Gwen limped over and put her arm around me. I couldn't tell if it was supposed to be comforting for me, or to help her balance. I didn't question it though. I liked it regardless.

Joey came out of the back with Miranda, who was now armed. "Nice going Kyle," he said sarcastically. "Now we are short a portal home. Let's go find one and go home."

I looked around at the damage we had caused to the Library of Congress. A burned table, numerous amounts of vines flung across the building. We had raised some sort of hell in this place.

CHAPTER 24

THE WITCH OF THE LEGION

As the five of us began to exit the Library we heard a slow clap from behind us. We each froze in our footsteps. No way in Hades could that have been Chrysaor. We killed him, or he killed himself. And we had kicked everyone else out of the building.

"Well done demigods. Or Bunker 4921, if that is how you'd rather be known as," I had turned around in search of the voice taunting us. Sitting on the edge of a railing was a teenage girl. She was impressive looking. Her hair was strewn back into a ponytail. But I had seen her before. This was the girl from the convenience store, and the warehouse. The Legion's little puppet, that the Inflictor was sent to recruit. Vivian had tracked us down.

"Vivian," I had snapped up to her.

Brian glanced at me then back at her, "Hold on broski. Let me try something." He turned towards Vivian and stepped forward looking up at her, "Why hello beautiful. Anything the son of the sun can offer you?"

I knew that was a mistake the second I heard him start that sentence. *Beautiful?* What was he trying to get her to like him? From what I knew of this girl, she was nothing he needed to be a part of.

Her eyes flicked towards him with bitterness. "Step back boy. The last boy I dated got killed by the Legion of Tartarus."

I smirked up and retorted, "You mean Hector? The boy you brought back to life and then dumped cause you wanted more power."

I had redirected her focus from Brian to me. I could see it in Joey and Gwen's eyes, how did I know so much about her?

"You seriously wish to test me, boy? How do you know of such occurrence anyways?" She narrowed her focus on me. I felt a buzzing sensation begin thriving through my mind. She opened her eyes and the buzzing had stopped. "The son of Poseidon. The one whom believes the prophecy is about him. The one who will cause hell to freeze over and kill the gods."

I froze in my place. I could see Joey having the others prepare for a fight. What she had just said struck me the wrong way. *The one whom believes the prophecy is about him.* This was yet another person telling me this. If it was not about me, who was it about?

Vivian had accomplished her goals. She got me too

awestruck to keep my mind clear. I got struck by one of her spells just like the Kapre tried to do at the diner.

My eye's fluttered and I swayed back and forth. Miranda and Gwen rushed to my side to help me from going out of consciousness. I refused to let that happen to me again.

Joey had a fierce look in his eye. He seemed to not want anything to do with this fight, but knew he must. If my suspicion held true, no I refused to think that way. He couldn't still be working with the Legion. He swore he was done.

"You demigods have failed. The Legion has already secured this book. It will be quite useful in your destruction. A book of incantations is something you really shouldn't give a child of Hecate."

Brian perked up, "You're kidding me right? Of course it makes sense. She found it second, after Miranda had found it. Go flipping figure."

Brian's ranting had bought me enough time to sneak away. Gwen and myself walked towards the staircase. We were out of view from the whacko spell caster.

I quickly whispered my plan to Gwen. "Gwen, do you trust my plan now?" I quizzically asked. I needed her help on this in order to stop the psycho witch.

"Kyle, this is one of your stupidest plans ever," she paused momentarily letting out an exasperated sigh. "But you are my best friend so I trust you. Go get 'em waterboy."

Gwen darted, with a limp, out from under the railing and sprung up three sets of vines. One around Vivian's waist, and two around her wrists.

Brian chuckled, "Now would you look at that! Just look at it. By the looks of it, I'd say you've just been, puppetfied."

Miranda picked up a broken table leg, "Brian, that isn't a word."

"Well, it is now. And Vivian is the first for it to be applied to."

"As a child of Wisdom, I can tell you that is not how it works, but whatever. We shall go with that for now. Vivian is now puppetfied. Happy?"

He cheered up grinning like a fool, and stupidly rejoiced, "Now this is a half-blood I can work with!"

A ball of fire blasted at his feet. I just needed Gwen to hold the vines a bit longer in order to take her out.

Just keep her distracted long enough Brian, I thought. I felt the water in the bathroom's pipes surge in my gut. It was like an ocean's tide. Pulling and pushing. Waiting to unleash the next big wave. The power of water truly was untamable.

And then I let it loose, and hell began to break loose as well. A stream of water began to surge towards me. I reached into it and grabbed a blade out of the water. I held it in my hand and clenched tightly around it's hilt. Ice began to trickle from my fingertips solidifying the blade. The water circled around me protecting me.

Vivian had turned her head to spot me as the bathroom doors had broken off of it's hinges. She turned to face me, combusting her hands to burn away the vines. Gwen winced in pain since her hands got burned from the flames trickling down the vine.

"Gwen!" I shouted in despair. Between her hands being burned, a concussion, and probably a broken leg I wasn't sure how much she would be able to take. "Joey, get Gwen to safety!"

Vivian flicked her wrist at the ground next to Gwen. A dark ominous portal began to swirl. It reminded me of the portals to the Realms, but much, much darker. A figure the size of an elephant began to arise from its depths.

My vision could no longer be focused over the railings. I needed to focus on my now advancing enemy, Vivian. My throat began to close. My friends were now in danger. We were going to all be wanted by United States Government as well for destruction of a national monument. Vivian's smile was crooked. "You know, for a half-blood of the Elder Olympian, especially of your stature."

I interrupted her, "Don't talk to me of my lineage. None of that matters. The only thing that I care about at this moment is you against me, and protecting my friends. You are only some power hungry selfish witch. You may be a demigod like me, Brian, Gwen, Joey, Miranda, and all the other half-bloods at Demigod Central, but you aren't one of us. You are working with the enemy."

Vivian began to chuckle. Her dark hair now draped past her shoulders ripped away from her ponytail. It began to look like a wild mess. As if she was in the woods for a few weeks on her own and her hair hadn't met a brush either in that time.

"You know what, Kyle. You are smart, but not smart enough. You and me are not the same. I am welcoming in the dawn of the Legion of Tartarus. I am choosing the side that will come out on top, and eventually you will too." She flicked her wrist down below towards Miranda.

A small blast sent Miranda and Brian flying backwards. Joey meanwhile was eyeing the beast that stood in front of him. It was blocking his path to Gwen. Brian had just shot an arrow into the beast's eye and it cracked like an eggshell.

I could hear him desperately mumble, "Oh c'mon, I've only got two arrows left."

As the casing of the monster cracked apart like an eggshell, sand began to pour from it's crevices. As its hands ripped the shell of it's head it revealed a sand golem.

"My arrow's are *not* going to work on that thing," Brian said in angst. He was becoming desperate. His personality would not let him fail his friends here. Brian walked closer towards the golem as Joey held its attention.

He split apart his bow into the two blades and pulled out his mask and slipped it on. "Por los dioses," he yelled while doing this and began a charge.

I quickly racked my brain. Did he just scream in Spanish; *for the gods?* I didn't feel like questioning it and rushed into combat with the daughter of Hecate.

My sword clashed against a purple beam cast out from her hand. I had to give Vivian credit. She had learned several strong spells and incantations through her training with the Legion. But I couldn't let her take this book again. If she got to learn all of it, she'd become one of the strongest magicians ever.

I began a volley of attacks. Sword, water, water, sword, more water. Each strike being countered. One misstep on my part and she'd be given a great target opportunity.

Her hand lit ablaze and forgot about her retreat. She clutched my wrist controlling the water, and it all splashed to the floor. "Foolish son of Poseidon. You seriously thought you could stop me alone. You think you've learned to control your abilities yet you can't even stop me."

I spied the book in her satchel. Now I just needed to get that from her. *Too late.* She had caught my eyes darting back and forth. I was like a caged otter. Not wanting to be caged. Just longing for the water. Her other hand reached and clenched my sword hands wrist. She began to push me towards the railing.

My back slammed against it. Her pursuit far from over. She stood almost on top of me glaring down on me. "It's over Kyle. The Legion is destined to win in the end anyways."

"You all may win in the end, but the end isn't today!" Gwen shouted, sprouting roots around Vivian's feet and hobbled closer.

"That's impossible I burned your hands, you were unconscious!" Vivian was flabbergasted. I smiled as I knew my chance was about to come.

"Next time you take someone on, make sure one of them does not have any healing powers." Gwen had a satisfied smirk on her face. She had totally owned Vivian and defeated her plan.

I realized my shot to take her out was now. I grabbed the book from her satchel and spun around the banister. I tossed the book down to Miranda while shouting out her name. I spotted Joey and Brian still focused on the sand golem.

I whirled the water up around her like a whirlpool. I began to freeze it from the bottom up.

"You think you've won, don't you two?" Vivian inquired.

"Well, by the looks of it, I'd say so," I retorted in confidence.

Vivian smiled, "Sometimes the magic is stronger than a simple half-blood trap, especially one learned from that book. The Fallen Hero shall await your arrival Kyle." She closed her eyes and began to mumble. When her eyes open they were pure purple.

The ice and vines began to melt and burn away from her. Vivian's whole body began to glow that tint of purple.

"Get away, and shut your eyes!" Joey screamed in desperation.

All of our eyes shut instantly, and a loud boom shook the room. I cautiously peeked open my eyes and realized she was gone. I looked over at Gwen and she gave me thumbs up that she was ok. I looked over the edge and saw Miranda hugging the book. Joey and Brian had a look of confusion on their faces as to where the sand monster had disappeared to.

Brian gave a disgruntled face, "Aw, I wanted to take Dune down."

Joey looked at him cross-eyed, "Who in Hades name is Dune?"

"You know that giant sand monster, thingy. I decided to name him Dune, since he is like a giant sand dune at a beach."

I helped Gwen down the steps and chided in, "That's not a bad name or comparison Brian. Good job! Still got the book Miranda?"

"Yeah," she said surprised. "It's all still here too. But all in all, we should get out of here now."

"Agreed," Gwen said weakly. "We need to get to the portals. Preferably before another attack happens here. I think we have done enough damage for one day."

CHAPTER 25

THE RISE OF A VIGILANTE

If getting attacked by a trained witch demigod who was hellbent on your destruction wasn't your cup of tee, or a golden swordsman, then I have no idea what is. I guess you like some peaceful stories involving cheesy monster-human romance. Well, boo you, because that wasn't my story at all.

As we cracked opened the door to the Library of Congress, we saw a swat vehicle was positioned in front of us as well as a couple dozen police vehicles waiting for us to emerge.

One of the officers had a megaphone and shouted into it, "Come out with your hands up! You all are trespassing on government property."

We looked at one another in confusion, and Brian finally spoke up, "I think they may have followed us from the Smithsonian, or maybe we tripped a silent alarm along the way?"

We looked at each other and shrugged. Gwen began to sit on a desk, "I can't run guys. Loki warned us only three could go. I'll stay behind."

Joey turned and stared her down, "No one is getting left behind. With Loki's logic only three of us could make it out of here. Well, now there is five of us. So what do you think of that? We are going to figure out our way out of here."

Brian smirked, "Kyle, pass me your backpack for a second."

"What, why?" I had no idea what he was planning on doing but any idea right now was probably a better idea than any idea we had at the moment.

He shuffled around the contents of my backpack and then finally gasped with excitement. His pitch almost sounded like a giddy school girl. "I found it. Yes! *Hehehe!*"

"What did you find?" Miranda asked confused by Brian's sudden excitement over this predicament.

He held a black with gold stitching piece of cloth. He put it on and surprisingly enough, Brian's outfit worked with the cloak. His jacket had a golden strip running down the arms of it and he wore dark jeans as well. He slipped the cloak over his head, and put on his mask and readied his bow.

I looked at him in awe. He truly looked like a vigilante, that goes on a mission, and becomes a hero in the end, kind of guy right now. "Call me Nightbow!" Brian said with a muffled and sarcastic sounding voice.

Joey and Gwen both looked at him like condescending

parents, "What the hell are you doing?!" They said it in unison and Miranda chuckled.

"I am going to be the hero here. And the only way for me to become a hero, is start out as the villain."

The villain, he had a point. Were any of us heroes here. Were we fighting a just fight?

Gwen looked at him, "That is the craziest plan I have ever heard, but it may just work in the long run."

"You see," Brian started. "My plan is that I go out there and confront them, or distract them. Either way it gives you all a way to escape and I take one-person hostage, they free that one. And maybe that is what Loki meant by only three can successfully leave the quest. We won't all be leaving here together, but meet up later on."

I looked around judging their faces, "I agree. No way we can all get out of here, Brian, *erh*, Nightbow's plan makes the most sense. He will become a hero, at least in our eyes.

He bowed as if gesturing a thank you. He grabbed an arrow and notched it at Miranda, "Sorry Miranda, but Loki said it was members of Bunker 4921, so this is our plan. C'mon. Go out the door."

She ushered herself forward and looked at me, "Your friend needs to be checked out after this is all over."

I shrugged, "Yea, I kinda figured. He is kinda losing his mind. Maybe its the jacket, or the mask."

"I said move!" Brian had an attitude towards everyone now. I began to wonder if this was his overall plan, if he never planned to go back to Demigod Central.

Brian guided Miranda with her hands over her head as she walked towards the door. She opened the door with her foot and the guards readied their guns.

"Don't shoot!" she exclaimed. "I was taken prisoner and I am being guided out right now. My assailant is behind me with an arrow pointed at my chest.

Brian walked onto the steps of the Library of Congress. I zipped up my backpack and walked over to Joey to help run with Gwen. Brian began to scream, "MY NAME IS NIGHTBOW! I am your new Vigilante, world. This girl was my get out safe card. I have three arrows around this block trained on her and will fire if I do not get out of here unscathed." He slipped something into Miranda's pocket.

The officer on the megaphone shouted back, "Kid, or uh, Nightbow, you realize you are taking a hostage, and you are lucky we haven't taken you down already. Release the girl and we will give you a head start."

"Really?"

"No, but we know you're still new at this to believe that kid."

Brian began to laugh like a mad man. A few of the officers began to eye one another expecting the worst. "Oh,

I am gonna have fun now, but remember, no killing. At least for now."

The megaphone officer cocked his head with confusion right before an arrow whizzed into the megaphone knocking it to the floor.

"Go time," Brian said. Then he whispered to Miranda, "Go get out of here and find the others."

The chaos Brian had started was enough for us to run down the steps while the police were distracted, and wait for him a few blocks away. We carried Gwen as she limped weakly, her ankle was worse than we had thought initially. She tried to do a light run on it, but instead looked like a little kid learning to walk. So we decided to keep on carrying her.

We found the little café that Miranda had told us about and we waited outside at a table for her and Brian.

Moments later a waitress showed up at our table, "Hi welcome to Barnaby's Café would you like to try a pastry of the day?"

Gwen looked at her, smiled and responded that she'd like to order five.

Joey scornfully looked at her, "I don't eat pastries."

"Who said they were for you. Ha-ha."

It was nice to see them joking around and not being

stressed out about escaping, although I knew it was just for show. Brian's odds of escaping were slim to none, but he didn't let us think of anything better than him making it out alive.

Just as all hope seemed lost of them rejoining us, Miranda turned the corner and joined us, "I am not sure if he will escape. His plan did not seem too safe."

I shook my head, "That's because it wasn't, it was planned as a suicide mission. A contingency plan the Bunker had in place."

Gwen looked at me like I was speaking a foreign language. "Fine, not the Bunker, but me and him. We agreed to always cover each others back's. And it included making that sacrifice if for the greater good of the mission."

We paused and all hung our heads low, not ready to move on and figure out what to do next.

Just then a voice spoke up, "Gods you all seem like you've just gone to like ten funerals. Gesh cheer up! And yeah, I'm alive."

We all ran over and gave him a hug. "So Nightbow lives to fight another day?" Gwen asked.

He smiled back, "You know it baby! So where is this portal nearby, that we did not use the first time!"

Joey looked at him, "I had to meet with an associate first Brian. You know that."

Brian slung his bow across his back, "Yeah." Brian's tone took a sarcastic tone and became more serious. "You know, I'm pretty positive that the associate was Morpheus!"

Miranda and Gwen awkwardly sat there watching the brothers begin a fight.

Joey's eyebrows kept ruffling. "Brian Schmitz, you are not permitted to talk about what you saw there, understand?"

"No, I don't understand why my brother has decided to go and work for the Legion."

"Enough Brian!" Joey began to roll up his sleeve. On it was a tattoo of the Legion of Tartarus' emblem, the skull with a knife through the eye. I was astonished at the sight of the tattoo. I knew it was there, but I had never truly made the connection before. The leader of the Bunker whom I had come to trust, had betrayed us. The skull's eyes seemed to pierce my body. I could feel Morpheus' words sting in my mind, "don't trust those closest to you kid, one day you'll get stabbed in the back by one."

Morpheus' words held true at this moment.

"Let me explain myself, before you all write me off," pleaded Joey. "I was young, and alone left to protect Brian, I did what I had to do. And if that meant joining some cult. I did it! I cut ties with them when I found out about Demigod Central though. Morpheus was in charge of me and my missions. So that is what I had to do. I had to officially resign so they would leave me alone."

Brian was shaking his head, "You gave me that mask when we first started doing missions. You made me a pawn of the Legion."

"I'm sorry Brian." Joey's voice was broken. He knew he had failed everyone on this journey. His past was catching up to him.

And Loki's little fire prophecy seemed to be coming full circle. We did not all make it out together. The portal landed us against the bay, so close enough to sea, and we did start as three. Brian decided to let Nightbow be known, but not how he had originally foreseen him as. And now Joey was facing his past.

The five of us made our way to the portal. We were all quite with the exception of Brian telling the story of escaping the police. He seemed happy which was good.

Once back at Demigod Central, we were quickly summoned to go to Headmaster Akhbar's office. Not much a hero's welcome back if you asked me.

CHAPTER 26

THE MEETING WITH AKHBAR

The three of us walked into the Headmaster Akhbar's room. We knew we were about to get in a butt ton of trouble due to the fact that we had brought back a demigod. This was a search and grab mission not a search for some demigod. But we brought Miranda back instead.

Sometimes doing the right thing involves getting in trouble, and well quite frankly you just got go with the punch you receive.

Headmaster Charles Akhbar stood in the corner in his slick black suit and his bald head gleamed as we walked into the room. "Sit, quickly and quietly," he said harshly. We did as he said and I felt the leather seat sink as though I was ready to hide inside of it. "So, you brought back a daughter of Athena and added her to your roster without permission. This puts you all at two now. I expected more from the elite's you all claim to be. Or is Bunker 4921 just a weak group that needs to be disbanded." Akhbar said this and a smirk crept across his face as he saw fear ring upon mine and Brian's face.

Joey stood up in protest, "You will never get away with doing anything like that Akhbar! Mainly because I won't let you!" Joey was one of the bravest demigods I had ever met, and the only one to ever stand up to the Headmaster like that. He didn't cower in fear or anything. He just stood there not afraid of anything.

"You dare to defy me Schmitz? Granted you did succeed in bringing back the Book of Shadows. You also proceeded return with some red headed daughter of Athena, or Minerva or whomever the goddess of wisdom she may be. It does not matter! And I do not simply have the time, matter, or reason to give two shits. You had failed now I presume you will need to pay a price for defying me just now Joseph Schmitz." I gulped as I looked at Joey who was mortified. "Kyle and Brian leave my office immediately. I need to speak with Joseph here on a matter of his manners. Next time finish a mission with more precision and less collateral damage."

Joey turned and put his arm on my shoulder, "Good luck Kyle. Don't be afraid of what the future holds. Continue to train your heart out and listen to Gwen. She will help you out a lot in the long run. And remember to help the twins continue their construction on those battle suits they wanted to build. You'll make one hell of a hero!"

"Joey, we will see each other again. You aren't going anywhere!"

"I wish I could agree with you, but I fear as though we

may not see one another for a while. Best of luck Kyle."

With that Brian dragged me out of the room and I could hear Akhbar yelling curses at Joey instantly after the door closed. I felt bad for Joey. It wasn't his fault at all. Chrysaor had gone after me. I had caused the issues with the authorities. I should be getting hashed at here, not Joey.

***

Time seemed to go on forever sitting in the Bunker. Brian sat twirling an arrow having the arrow head press against his finger. Gwen sat at the table with Miranda and Nicole. She was wrapping her hands with cloth. Her hands still had not fully healed since meeting Vivian. Her head was healing, and her ankle was in a brace.

Jim and Tim sat arguing with one another over how to design the mech suit they were building.

I paced back and forth staring at the pages of the Book of Shadows. I flipped the pages and tried to make out the squiggles on the page. It looked like gibberish mixed with Pig Latin.

Just then the elevator dinged. As the doors opened Joey stood there with his head lowered. Behind him stood Chiron, Akhbar, and Hecate. *Not good!*

But that wasn't my first thought. The first thought I had was, *how does Chiron fit in the elevator with them? The elevator isn't that big.*

The four paraded out and Hecate stared at me advancing towards me. "My oh my, Kyle Pierce you have saved my ass from Athena's wrath."

"What?" Joey asked the goddess.

"You see, I had borrowed the book. My dear friend Dolos, the apprentice of Prometheus, spirit of tricksters. Yeah well, he persuaded me to borrow the book from Athena's Collection to let him browse upon it."

Miranda approached the goddess, "You mean to tell me you stole the Book of Shadows, to give to a spirit, who is known to work for a head honcho of the Legion of Tartarus?"

Hecate shrugged, "Kind of."

I slammed the book shut. "Chiron, what do you want us to do, give the book to the goddess who has wavered on her faith in the gods to support the Legion, or hold onto it until we can find the Book of Wisdom and whatever else may be missing from Athena's library."

Chiron stated, "Kyle it is best we-"

"Hold onto the Book of Shadows Bunker 4921," Akhbar began.

"I'm sorry did Akhbar just support us?" Brian asked in confusion.

I glanced over at Gwen. She was tensing up, uncertain of

what to make of this situation.

Akhbar began to speak again, "My role of Headmaster is to support my students, and you are students under my jurisdiction. But, when action is done in the wrong discourse, I also need to take action. That is why I regret to inform you that Joey Schmitz, was asked to leave Demigod Central."

I noticed as he said this his shirt collar had fallen slack a bit. Some sort of marking was on Akhbar's neck. It reminded me of the mark of the Legion, but it wasn't like Joey's. He saw me eyeing his neck and fixed his collar.

"Woah!" Brian exclaimed, "You can't do that. It's not fair. Is there nothing we can do? Can't we get a three strike rule and then you're out?"

Nicole eyed our Headmaster and spoke up, "Charles Akhbar, you have the attention of our Bunker. And even though he has proved to be a lack luster leader to myself, I will vouch that he does not deserve to be kicked off our Realm."

Akhbar rubbed his chin. "Three strikes could be Nicole, Miranda, and your prior quest with the Karkadann. There is your three."

"I'm going with him," Brian slowly said. "Guys, it's fine. We failed you, so now we will take the fall."

Joey raised his lowered head, "Brian, I can't expect you to

go with me. This is your home."

"Nope, home is with you, you big dummy."

Akhbar spoke up once more, "Your bags are packed. I will see you all will find the gate appropriately. Joey you have time to say your goodbyes at the gate. And Brian you will be missed."

Hecate, Akhbar, and Chiron walked to the elevator. "Wait Chiron," I called out. "I need to talk to you for a moment."

"About?" he quizzically asked as Akhbar and Hecate boarded the elevator.

The two of us walked to a back room of the Bunker. "Before leaving, I had a dream. I had seen Chrysaor, and Vivian. Then once we had left, I fell asleep searching through my mind for anything about Chrysaor. As it turns out that I had connected to his mind. I relived his troubled past. He trained under you, did you know he would turn out evil, yet train him regardless?"

"Yes," Chiron said lowering his head. "I train demigods. He was still half-god. So he was a half-blood. I do not have a preference. I like to think I am training heroes, and they will fight the just fight. Chrysaor had a vendetta to settle. He couldn't in the end. And he was enraged."

I thought of the idea, "Do some heroes still turn out bad?"

"They can, if given the right motive, they can shift morals.

Their view becomes corrupted by a false hope. I fear some others may have it occur soon as well."

He began to trot away and I looked at him with despair, "Hey, one last thing. Chrysaor when he was training Vivian mentioned something about a fallen hero. And that the Inflictor is chasing after him. I think I may know who it is."

"Really, that is good news than. Who is he?"

"I think it is Vivian's ex-boyfriend, Hector."

Chiron pondered the idea. "Once we have another lead on it, we may send out another quest. After all, you all are the best of the best. Keep up the good work in the Bunker. Especially with the new leadership." He walked to the elevator and left.

I was left alone in the Bunker now. I sat looking around remembering the memories I had with Gwen, Brian, and Joey. Now the four of us who had truly started the Bunker was cut in half. It was time I said my farewell.

CHAPTER 27

A BITTERSWEET FAREWELL

I walked to the edge of campus. The portal to the Realms sat in front of us. The doorway was etched like an ancient Mayan stone structure. Joey and Brian both had their hands full with their bags. Brian had only a look of distress on his face. He didn't have to go with Joey, but he was making his own choice here to stick with his brother, wherever their journey took him.

His decision to leave was hitting me hard.

Jim and Tim both ran over to hug the Schmitz brothers goodbye. Joey was handing them each a present, while saying his farewells to the troublesome duo.

"You shouldn't be so tough on Brian, Kyle. He is only doing what he believes is right." Gwen clasped my shoulder while saying this to me. Her touching me sent a jolt down my spine. Her ankle was still in a brace from the Library of Congress. I was almost hoping she wouldn't be here right now.

I turned my head back at her and glared deeply. "Gwen,

I really don't think you get this. He just got up and is willing to walk away from all of this like it was nothing. He could've stayed. He should've. He doesn't need to follow Joey around like a little puppy dog. It is time for him to be his own person."

Gwen shook her head, "Kyle you are self-absorbed. Maybe Brian is needed in the real world right now for a reason that doesn't involve you. Just because you have a prophecy around you does not mean the world revolves around Kyle."

"I'm starting to think I don't Gwen. Not the world. Not the prophecy. None of it. Chrysaor and Vivian both said it. I don't think I am important as everyone is making me out to be."

"Whatever Kyle, our friends are leaving now and I am going to say goodbye. We can talk about this later." She pushed her way forward to say her farewells to Joey.

Brian looked at me and gave the smirk he always had. Except this time, it was more empty. Half-hearted almost like he was wanting to say goodbye at the same time. I tried to find a smirk to send one back to him. But quite frankly I was too mad to do anything else. I was being selfish, maybe I was like Narcissus in a way, Gwen may have been right. I wasn't caring that my friend was leaving and I most likely would not see him anytime soon. And maybe it was for the best.

"Pierce, get over here already!" Joey was shouting for me

to join him. Maybe, just maybe I could muster up enough strength here to hear what he had to say. Maybe it was my promotion, to leader of the Bunker.

"Yeah," I said jogging over. "What did you need to say?"

Joey looked at me like I had three heads, "Uhm, I was going to say my farewell till we meet again. But you know we don't have to, if you don't want to."

I paused a kicked some of the dirt around, "Well, I didn't mean it like that."

"Get over here already." He gave me a huge hug and cracked my back.

"*Ack-*" wincing and gasping for breath, "Oh that actually felt not too bad." I paused for a moment trying to figure out how I wanted to formulate my next thought.

"So Joey, with you leaving and all, who are you going to hand over leadership to? Like I know I need a little bit more training in my leadership class, but I finish the class at the end of the semester." I looked at him sternly, "I'm not liking the sound of the silence."

He chuckled then ruffled my hair, "Kyle, bud, I couldn't promote you to leader. I gave it to Gwen. She is now the leader of Bunker 4921."

Brian was chuckling, "Man Kyle, bet you weren't expecting that rug pulled out from under you." His laughing was getting to me. Gwen was sitting there all pretty with a flower resting in her braided hair. My hand clenched into a fist. My other hand slowly became a fist as well, and I prepared a strike.

Brian saw my intentions and jumped in front of Joey grasping my arm as it lunged for Joey. My other fist made contact with Brian, and Joey frantically backed off. Gwen stepped forward reaching for her side but she was unarmed.

"The role should have been mine! We were brothers Brian! We-" I was cut off from my rant when Brian caught me with a cross to the jaw.

I began to pick myself up and wipe the blood from my lip. Brian looked down at me ready to strike again. "We were brothers Kyle, but by the looks of it, not any more." He turned his back to me and walked towards Joey.

Chiron cantered over to us, as well as several guards. I closed my eyes and unclenched my fists. I had been the one to turn my back on Joey here, this is all my fault now. I had brought this upon myself now, and now the consequences would be mine to face.

Now I stood alone in the end. Loki's prophecy had come full circle. Joey was the one to face his past. Brian made a sacrifice of compromising his identity as Nightbow. And now I had betrayed my friends and stood alone. The prophecy had to do with us and nothing about the book.

Chiron began to shout in his worried voice, which he had almost always, "What has happened here? Can there not be a goodbye without a fight. Mr. Grant Underhill please escort our friend to his dorm room. I will talk to you later Kyle."

Grant was big burly guy who had a couple years on me. He usually stood post guarding the doors. He was the son of Ares so he definitely could. He was actually our head doorman/guard. He had the passages secured tighter than the Hercules and Heracles kids.

He pushed me forward to get me to walk some, "Keep it moving kid. I'm not pleased of what I am tasked to do here, but I must."

I had looked up at him trying to draw recognition. I had seen that same line written in the Inflictor's diary on the day he recruited Vivian. However, I could not place Grant, with the Inflictor. Maybe it was just a common phrase that I hadn't heard all that often.

I was drawn back to reality with a slight push to my back from Grant, "Keep walking."

I looked back once I got to the door to look at Joey and Brian one last time. I would miss the two. However, I believed I had distanced myself enough from them to not see them for some time. Though I would miss them, I would also be ok with that.

CHAPTER 28

MY EPILOGUE

Grant left me once we got to my floor and he returned to his post at the front door or the Grand Hall. I began to walk to my room and I stopped when I saw Brian's name no longer on the door next to mine. I sighed heavily and opened the door.

Inside, it was strange, the dorm was empty and dark. I was upset that Brian had left and moved out. There was a photo Brian had left on my bed nook. It was the two of us outside of the Lincoln Memorial where we had just talked to the know-it-all red headed girl, that had told the tour guide all the wrong facts. We had celebrated our journey thus far by taking a photo. Then Chrysaor had to ruin everything.

I stared at the photo Brian, Miranda, Gwen and myself and tossed it aside.

In my mind it was still funny seeing that girl embarrass the tour guide. I'm glad we had brought Miranda back with us. It showed that we still could help people out even if it wasn't the desired task.

I picked up the photo once more and I placed it on Brian's bed. Or no one's bed now. Since Brian and Joey had left on bad terms with the Headmaster, and now myself. I changed into my pajamas and laid on my bed. I believed that my dreams would finally subside and be normal. Only if that was a possibility. Alas, it was not the case, nor ever was.

***

I was walking behind a tall man who was wearing a black suit and had a red flower in his suit. His skin was tan and he had his black hair slicked back like a hockey player's. He opened the door and it creaked eerily. He closed the door behind him and took a seat at the end of the table.

The other end of the table was a being, darker than darkness itself. There were two others in the middle of the table but they sat motionless with the only motion coming from either of them was their breathing.

The other end of the room was absorbing darkness into an abyss. Some sort of void of a life form was at the other end. It was sucking in the shadows of the room. The void began to speak in a dark raspy growl, "So, did the boy accept your offer during his quest?"

The man with his hair slicked back paused and shifted uncomfortably in his shoes. He finally spoke, but although he was scared he had confidence in his voice, "He denied the offer to join the Legion. However, we have set the great prophecy in motion. The boy has become aware of his fate and he will have to face his greatest fear in due time. When time comes Poseidon will not be able to save him and he must fight for himself. With that centaur, Chiron training him he will not stand a chance. This boy will need experience and skill, not luck. He won't even acquire any of the skills he needs either. Fear not my liege."

The man in the middle pounded his fist on the table, "Damn you Morpheus! You had one god forsaken job, Morpheus!"

Another figure at the middle of the table stood up. A cracked helmet glinted with shines of brightness that were immediately sucked into the void. "I died for nothing then. To be sent back here in a fragile form, for you to have just let him keep the book!"

Chrysaor's voice was directed towards one of the two figures sitting across from him. It wasn't soon before all the participants at this meeting were throwing one another under the bus.

The void grumbled across the room, "Silence, all of you!"

Morpheus tensed his fist, "Listen here you little worthless shit of a half-ling. I'm working my ass off to set this prophecy in motion ahead of its time. Sending the boy on the quest was required in order to advance our progress. Without progress we are set to regress. If you had included Prometheus in this meeting I'm sure he would agree. Give it two years' tops and I promise you. No, I swear to you on the throne of all the Olympians that you will be rising from this abyss you reluctantly call home."

The void looked right at me. It was a man darker than darkness. It was an essence. Hardly able to be a being, it was struggling to maintain a form. "The boy is in this meeting Morpheus! You've invited him here to listen to this fight against my doing! For that you will feel my wrath. You have been trusted, but alas no longer. Time for you to learn you are a lesser member of this Legion and nothing more but a henchman to do my bidding. I can easily find another. One who will prove you are nothing more than a faded god!"

With that being said, the void reached out dissolving the scene. Morpheus had tried to warn me, but of what?

I had remembered Morpheus from our little encounter at the Washington D.C. headquarters for the Legion. Morpheus was against us, but seemed like he was with us at the same time. He was playing both sides trying to help.

I shook in my bed with a cold sweat. I must have hit my panic alarm on my night stand because Jim and Tim were breaking through my door, with the help of Gwen. They rushed to my bed and Gwen cradled me in her arms.

Chiron galloped through the hallway shouting at nearby kids to get out of his way. He came into my room and looked at my shocked state. He came to my side and shined a flashlight into my eyes. "Kyle what is wrong. What did you see in your dream?"

I nodded my head and he understood who was the root of it. "Morpheus. He showed you something didn't he?"

I sat up reluctantly in my bed as Gwen let go and let her arm drape across my shoulder. I gulped down the frog in my throat so I could open my mouth and speak. "Morpheus showed me a room inside of Tartarus. And three men were there besides him. The dark being saw me and knew who I was, that I would be of some importance in some prophecy, that would awaken him. Chrysaor was there as well. Morpheus let us keep the book. What is this prophecy about exactly? You've told me I'm in one, but I think it's time I know what this is all about," I asked in a panic.

He looked at me sternly, "The prophecy speaks of our doom, Kyle. The destruction of everything we have come to cherish and love. And almost all of it is at your hand."

Doom, I began to wonder if I was not meant to be the hero but the villain like Chrysaor and Vivian had said.

Rusty Wissman III

THE
LEGION
AWAITS...

COMING SOON:

HALF-BLOOD ORIGINS BOOK 2:

LANCE WAKEMAN AND THE FALLEN HERO

THE UNWANTED TRAVELER

Time was of the essence. Sweat beaded across my face as I quickly tried to break the security code protecting the computer. No luck, the computer was protected too tightly to be unwound like a simple wristwatch. I could hear footsteps down the hall of a guard coming my way. I had run out of time, and luck at that. Luck was never a strong point of mine.

I sprinted down the hall way and as I turned a corner I completely wiped out. I had failed to see the wet floor sign on the ground in the dimly lit hallway. I tried to scamper up to my feet but it was pointless now.

The guard approached me with his handcuffs and badge and shackled my hands together. Well, there goes my plan of hacking into the Manticore Global computer system. Not my brightest idea. Heck, I didn't even know what the hell Manticore Global was! How about I go to the beginning to how I got here and explain a little bit of what is going on to you.

***

My name is Lance Wakeman, and I am 17 years old. I

have short blonde hair and bluish grey eyes. I am just about 6 feet tall. I hail from the outskirts of Washington D.C. on the Maryland side of the beltway in a small town called Silver Spring. My GPA is a 5.29, and I am one of, if not, the smartest kids in my school. And for some reason if there is a sign that says restricted and there is technology involved, I need to break the rules.

My Dad is a local police officer who often bails me out of my arrests, or saves me from the cops sent to arrest me. I got lucky to have a dad to save my ass from time to time. My mom on the other hand, well she had left us after my birth and I never had the pleasure of meeting her. My dad tells me I have her eyes and smile and that I look just like her. Personally, I have nothing to compare it to, not even a photo of her, so I just smile and nod to please my dad.

It was 9 o'clock on a Friday night. All offices were closed and everyone had gone home. Wait, I should go back even further than that for better clarification here.

Earlier in the day some bullies at my school had dared me to steal information on a file named *HEROES*. It took them a little bit of persuading to get me to accept their terms, but I was easily persuaded after I took a couple blows to the gut and getting slammed into the lockers.

"Wakeman!" Freddy shouted holding my shirt to the locker.

"Oh c'mon, Freddy. Not today guys, I don't have any lunch money today," I whined hoping not to get a usual.

And by usual I mean an ass whooping. Those were definitely not a fan favorite of mine.

"Look Lance, my friends here need your assistance in the computer area. They are, *uh, uh.*" Freddy paused thinking of the word.

"Wow Freddy, how on Earth did you ever get past Freshman year of high school? Actually no, I know exactly how, they want you out of here sooner than latter."

"Wakeman!" he said, throwing a punch into my gut.

"*Ack gah, ah.*" I said, which still rings pain into my ears writing it down.

Freddy pointed to three friends of his behind him. "These boys right here are in search of your expertise. And lucky for you, I'm in a good mood since they are paying nicely."

There was that word again, *luck*. I'm not a lucky person. Why do people keep thinking I am?

I looked at his new buddies. I spotted a skull tattoo with, what was that, a knife? Going through it's eye. Weird, I thought to myself, who gets a tattoo in high school.

"So what expertise of mine do you need?" I asked the taller tattooed individual.

He opened his mouth but it was a bunch of clicks, groans, and the occasional moan thrown in.

After the kid said that, I looked at Freddy with confusion. "*Uhm*, what do they need me to do? All I got out of that was *ah-da-bup-a gra-uch*. More or less. Sorry my Tasmanian Devil is a bit rusty at the moment."

Freddy looked at me like I was stupid, "What part of computer skills do you not get. They need you to break into someplace, and retrieve these files for them. They prefer print copies for some reason."

"Impressive Freddy! That's the most I've heard you speak in a full sentence. It wasn't bad either. Don't hurt yourse-" I was pushing my luck as I took another blow to the gut. "Got you, break into this place, get the files, and deliver them on Monday."

"Eh, no worry Wakeman. Plus, you're getting out of an ass kicking by doing this for them. I'll give you a week off. Also, it's not like you have anything to do later. Unless you had some date, even though you have no friends."

Ouch, way to remind me on that one Freddy. Sad thing though was he was right. I was one of the most socially awkward kids at my school. My dad always says it is just a phase, or that it's puberty. Yeah, thanks dad. Puberty is the cause of your son getting bullied!

"I actually had a date with me and my games tonight. I told my controller I was gonna spend the whole night with her."

He stood there astonished for a moment, "You have a

226

girlfriend?"

"God no! Freddy c'mon, it's me. Closest thing to I have of a friend is you." As I gave him a slight awkward punch to the arm.

He chuckled. "I'm not your friend. You're my punching bag." He threw one last blow to my ribs and walked away.

I unfolded the piece of paper he handed me. Manticore Global, Silver Spring, MD. Folder *HEROES*, and any of it's contents. I crumpled the piece of paper and put it in my cargo shorts. I trekked my way towards class.

Ok, now back to 9 P.M. on this Friday night.

***

So after the last guard before the night shift made his last tour and his way to his car, I tossed a little stone I had found into the doorway.

It had actually worked and the door didn't catch on its lock.

I swiftly made my way through the door and pulled out the stone and slipped it back into my pocket. Now luckily the room I wanted to find was all the way in the back, so hopefully no one would see that any lights were on. I made my way to the main computer and once it had booted up is where my troubles began to occur. I only had five guesses to guess the computer's password or else the alarm would go off and I would be in trouble.

First try, no success. Likewise, was the case for my second, third, and fourth guesses. I needed some sort of luck to save myself now. One guess left, let's make it a good one, I had thought to myself. Luckily the fifth try was right.

My jaw dropped with excitement. I had thought I was screwed right then and there upon hitting enter. But somehow the password guessing trick I knew had pulled through for me. Did I actually have luck?

I quickly looked around the desktop and server files for a codename *HEROES*. No such luck. But then again, who would be dumb enough to put a top secret file on their desktop.

I searched about three more times, in harder to find places until one file folder came up. And I decided to click on it.

The first file was titled *William Parker*. As I read through it I found out it was just a kid. He was my age. What I was more curious about was his history section of the document, blank with one exception. A recording of an incident in Washington D.C. a few months ago detailing a report of causing a disturbance on the National Mall and Library of Congress.

Besides that, nothing was printed under him other than a name and a place of residence, New York, New York.

Why would they have an innocent kid listed in Manticore Global for no reason under his own codename file? Scanning through his information more I finally found another odd connection. Someone who I can guarantee he never had any contact with in his life a *Kyle* with no last name supplied and no point of origin. An even better file was *Brian "Nightbow" Schmitz*. Still under him, no information except a number, 4921.

Something was up. These files were here for a reason, and I couldn't let those kids from school get access to it. It was bad enough I did what they beat me up to do.

I printed out a copy, and simultaneously copied files to a ghost drive I always carried on me. I then tried to hack into other intel to see what I could dig up. And let's just say that I ran out of five tries and that is how I'm in my current predicament.

The usual occurrence happened. Sirens wailed.

I tried to run and make an escape. Let's just say I failed horribly. Luck was just teasing me there, I wasn't lucky. I fell on my face at some point. Got hand cuffed and then get escorted out. What made all of this worse, my dad was the one who had caught me.

As I took my "death march" as I like to call the walk of shame I noticed something that usually would not be seen, a man about 8 feet tall. Me only being 5 foot 11, I knew he was tall. I liked to say I was six foot tall, but I'm only 5'11". He was staring at me watching intently. The press was all lined up, and he hid well enough in their ranks. Except for his height.

Something else I took into consideration was that I could not make out his torso or feet. Not just because he was behind people, but I just couldn't see them. I heard him grunt and then snort almost horse like but I dismissed the idea. He must have been really drunk to be snorting like that in public. But with that you heard a loud screeching sound. The wailing got closer and it was a group of creatures limping, but sprinting closer and closer. They were after me.

My dad pushed me to the side as chaos broke out. And to think we were only 20 steps from the car.

He drew his gun and ordered the creatures to freeze.

Meanwhile, the giant man pulled up a camera and got a picture of me staring straight into his lens. Whoever that guy was he was up to no good at least to my liking.

As I looked back one of the wailing creatures had gotten closer to me and my dad yelled, "Don't move another step or I'll shoot!"

I paused thinking of the noise. It sounded like the kid from earlier with the skull tattoo. The tattoo that seemed to draw your attention.

Once I caught a glimpse of the face, I had recognized him immediately or it; it was one of the kids from earlier in my day that was with Freddy. They had planned for me to get caught after getting the files. My dad was there because he had been called, which was an advantage for my sake.

If the thing had a brain to concentrate it looked completely clueless. It just froze and adjusted its gaze from me to my dad. It glared its rotten teeth and bared them towards my dad. It screeched again and ran towards my dad. It wasn't as much of a run as it was a gallop.

The next thing I heard was three shots; *POP! POP! POP!* And the creature that was running towards him collapsed viciously onto the ground. The creature had translucent skin and you could make out its bones.

It appeared to be a skeleton or zombie like creature that just remained motionless. No blood came from its head or anything. I slowly got back to my feet and whispered, "Thanks dad." But apart from that, most of my shouts and screams were, "*Woah!* No not cool, not cool. Ah get it away!" But yeah, I'm trying not to sound so scared.

As we made our way up the others were leaving their fallen comrade alone. I guess the sight of him dead on the ground had them concerned. Or they went to go call in backup.

"No problem Lance, but you got to be more careful and a lot less stupid. Now let's get you home."

I quickly picked up my backpack and looked around. All the reporters were gone now, same as the tall man who managed to get a picture of me.

I got into my dad's car. We drove home in his undercover cop car, a 2011 Camaro. Personally, I'm not allowed to say this on the record, but I've "borrowed" this car a couple of times. Let's just say when my dad found out it would usually result in me having to clean up the basement. And by basement, I mean his own personal evidence locker for cases my dad would look into the supernatural occurrences.

Our little skeleton bully thing from my school was in the trunk of his car and likely to end up in the basement as well.

Then for some reason I thought about the man who took my picture. Who was he that he had a head on everybody else and why did he want my picture.

Now back in reality I caught the tail end of my dad's lecture, "You need to be more careful and a lot less like your mother."

Something he never mentions when I do wrong, my mom. I sat there and stared at him for a few seconds trying to fathom what he just said. Without thinking I blurted out, "Who is she exactly?"

I sounded like a little whinny two-year-old kid whimpering to him. He quickly snapped back to his old military self and murmured, "That's classified and you know it. Topic closed! Forget I even mentioned her Lance."

"No, this is not the military, and this topic is *not* closed. I demand information on her now!" This was the first time I had raised my voice at him in a while.

He came to a hard stop in the road as the Camaro drifted

some to its side taking up two lanes now. I heard the body slam against the back of the trunk.

"You can either shut the hell up right now, or you can walk home. Your choice, son."

"Fine, I'll shut up!"

"Aw I was hoping you would pick the second option. I like a good traveler," chimed in a voice from my dad's backseat.

My dad parked the car and turned to our unwanted traveler and said, "I'm sorry but who the hell are you, sir?"

"I'm the man in charge of travelers. And I need my nephew's assistance of course."

"Wait nephew?" I asked. "You mean me? Dad you had a brother?"

"No, I'm an only child. How are you related to my son?"

"Why I am his mother's brother of course. I am Hermes, the god of Travelers, and you my boy are needed by me, and the other gods. And what you just shot, and also have in your trunk is a Revenant. They are a zombie like creature that haunt people, and usually won't perish until their task is complete. So, if you don't mind Captain Wakeman, or whatever your police rank is, I need to borrow your son for an indefinite amount of time."

"No, you cannot take him. Not to your world! Not to the

place your sister showed me!"

"Ah but see this is different. A place for his kind where you will be safe from the harm he brings you." With that Hermes put his arm on my shoulder and I blacked out, and knew I wasn't in my dad's car anymore. I could tell my dad was furious. And I would most definitely be grounded when I returned home.

ABOUT THE AUTHOR

Rusty Wissman III grew up in Bowie, Maryland.
Which is a town well placed between Washington D.C.,
Annapolis, and Baltimore, Maryland. He grew up
loving mythology but always found his hardest class to
be my English class. Now it is one of his favorite
classes. He is currently enrolled at Mount St. Mary's
University and is pursuing a degree in Criminal Justice.
Aside from beginning to create this world in 8th grade,
he enjoys playing sports such as baseball and ice
hockey. He currently plans to create a series out of
Half-Blood Origins by following up The Book of
Shadows, with a story that sparked the idea for this
novel, Lance Wakeman and the Fallen Hero.